"Are you afraid of me?" Hammond mocked

"I—I think I'm more afraid of—of myself," she whispered. "I came simply because I wanted to be with you, but now I think perhaps I should go."

His hands snaked with lightning swiftness around her wrists. "You could run from me, but you can't run from yourself, Abbey." His fingers trailed a seductive path up her left arm, making her skin come alive responsively. Then his hand was at the nape of her neck, and he was forcing her head relentlessly toward his.

"I suggest you give yourself the opportunity of discovering exactly what you came here for."

Her lips quivered in fearful anticipation as she stared into his narrowed mocking eyes.

"Hammond..." she heard herself protest weakly, but his mouth was already sliding over hers to silence her in a devastatingly effective way.

YVONNE WHITTAL
is also the author of these

Harlequin Presents

and these

Harlequin Romances

Many of these books are available at your local bookseller.

For a free catalog listing all titles currently available,
send your name and address to:

HARLEQUIN READER SERVICE
1440 South Priest Drive, Tempe, AZ 85281
Canadian address: Stratford, Ontario N5A 6W2

YVONNE WHITTAL

bitter-sweet waters

Harlequin Books

TORONTO • NEW YORK • LOS ANGELES • LONDON
AMSTERDAM • PARIS • SYDNEY • HAMBURG
STOCKHOLM • ATHENS • TOKYO • MILAN

Harlequin Presents first edition December 1982
ISBN 0-373-10558-4

Original hardcover edition published in 1982
by Mills & Boon Limited

CHAPTER ONE

'I'M not looking forward to this,' Abbey Mitchell confessed silently to herself as she flung a few last-minute things into her suitcase and fastened the catches. Her employer had been kind enough to give her the Friday afternoon off, and Derek would be calling for her within the next half hour to take her home, to Sweet Waters, for the weekend, but she was wishing suddenly that he was taking her at least a million miles in the opposite direction.

Abbey had wanted a quiet engagement with only the family to share in the joyous occasion, but her mother would not hear of it, and Derek's parents had backed Claire Mitchell in this respect. It had to be a lavish affair with something close to a hundred guests to witness the event, and it had to be held out at Sweet Waters. After all, Abbey thought a little cynically, Sweet Waters possessed a dining-room as large as a banquet hall with doors leading conveniently out on to the wide terrace and sloping lawns. There was, in fact, enough room to accommodate twice as many people as were invited, but it was not exactly what Abbey had had in mind for herself and Derek, and her lovely mouth curved with displeasure.

She seated herself on the corner of her bed and stared down at her hands a little absently. Her hands were small, the fingers slender, and the nails tinted a delicate, subdued pink. In a little over twenty-four hours Derek would be placing his ring on her finger, and she felt happy and contented at the thought, except for one thing; the tremendous fuss which usually accompanied such an occasion, and Claire Mitchell was known for her elaborate functions.

Abbey sighed audibly as she rose to her feet, and her slender body moved with an unconscious grace as she crossed the room to stare out of her bedroom window down into the busy street below. The sound of the Durban traffic was muted, and her eyes, a clear blue beneath dark, perfectly arched brows, gazed blankly down at the jostling crowds on the pavement across the street. Beyond the tall buildings the Indian Ocean lay shimmering invitingly beneath the cloudless sky, offering a welcome relief from the humid heat which was fast becoming oppressive as summer approached, but Abbey was not tempted in that moment as her thoughts drifted.

She had known Derek Halstead for eighteen months. They had met shortly before her twenty-first birthday, and ever since then he had done his best to persuade her into marriage, but Abbey had been reluctant to tie herself down. She had a good job as private secretary in an architectural firm, she had a beautiful flat overlooking the city with its stretch of golden beaches, and her fast little car took her wherever she wanted to be. She had enjoyed her freedom while she had it, knowing that the time would come when she would have to think of settling down, but she had been in no hurry.

Abbey had known several men before Derek had come into her life, but none of them had lasted very long. They had found her beautiful, with her flowing black hair, heavily-lashed eyes, and delicately sculptured features, but the friendship had always ended abruptly when they had sought intimacies which her rigid upbringing had prevented her from allowing. Derek had been different, and more persistent in his courtship. He was twenty-eight, six years older than Abbey, but not once had he given the slightest indication that he had been more interested in a sexual relationship with her.

This was, perhaps, one of the reasons why she felt so attracted to him. Derek came from a wealthy, influential family, and he was working his way up in his father's engineering firm. He loved horses, and enjoyed the races when he was in need of excitement, but he made it quite clear from the start of their friendship that he was interested in marriage only. He loved her, he had said, intellectually as well as physically, and he could wait for the latter until after their marriage.

A smile lifted the corners of Abbey's mouth. After a spate of boy-friends with nothing but sex on their minds, Derek had been like an intriguing oddity at first. It was true that, intellectually, they were on the same level, and in his company she had found that she could breathe easier. She could lower her guard, and be herself, and it had been a comfortable feeling. He had accepted the fact that she needed time to make sure of her feelings for him, and he had waited with a remarkable show of patience until she had been ready to bind herself to him in marriage.

The doorbell rang, intruding shrilly on her thoughts, and she went to answer it as quickly as she could. It would be Derek, she knew that, and when she opened the door a familiar warmth filled her heart as she stared up at the tall, fair-haired man with the smooth, attractive features. He was far too good-looking, she had told him once in jest, and he had coloured with embarrassment. She had found it sweet, but she had never mentioned his appearance again, and as she looked at him now she could not help thinking that she was to be envied.

Derek smiled, white teeth flashing in his tanned face, then she was in his arms, and he was kissing her with

his usual restraint while she rested against him contentedly.

'We have a three-hour journey ahead of us,' he
reminded her at length. 'Are you ready to leave?'

'My suitcase is packed,' she smiled up into his warm
brown eyes, and fifteen minutes later they were caught
up in the city traffic, heading towards her home in the
Drakensberg.

Derek's Mercedes was air-conditioned and comfortable, making the journey a pleasurable experience on
that hot October afternoon, and Abbey leaned back in
her seat, relaxed and pleasantly drowsy when at last they
left the city behind them.

'Are you happy?' Derek asked, his hand finding hers
in her lap, and squeezing it gently.

'Oh, yes,' she sighed, her fingers curling about his.

'I've waited a long time for this day,' he said, removing his hand and taking his eyes briefly off the road to
glance at her. 'Are you going to make me wait as long
before you set the wedding date?'

'I think we can wait three months, don't you?'

Derek's eyes were faintly humorous as he slanted
another quick glance at her, but he could not disguise
that hint of eagerness in his voice as he asked, 'You
wouldn't perhaps consider changing that to three
weeks?'

'That's much too soon,' she protested laughingly, 'and
I'd like to enjoy what's left of my freedom.'

'Then I'll settle for three months, if that's what you
want,' he sighed resignedly.

'My mother will want an elaborate affair,' she
reminded him, 'and three months should be long enough
for her to make the necessary arrangements.'

'You sound as if you don't agree with your mother's
plans.'

'I don't,' she admitted, her beautiful mouth curving once more with deep displeasure. 'I would much rather have a quiet wedding somewhere without all the pomp and ceremony attached to it.'

'We could always slip away somewhere and let them know when it's all over,' Derek suggested lightly, but she shook her head and laughed, knowing that, at heart, he was a stickler for doing things according to the book.

'Can you imagine the unholy furore our families would create if we did something like that?'

'I can imagine,' he remarked drily. 'Taking everything into consideration it would perhaps be wiser to leave things as they are.'

They lapsed into silence, and Abbey actually dozed, but she awakened with a pleasurable start when they turned off at Estcourt, taking the Bergville road to Sweet Waters which was situated at the foot of the mighty Drakensberg mountains with its majestic peaks and deep, lush valleys. They were coming closer to her home, the place she had loved so intensely as a child, but the city had called with its prospects for the future, and she had left the farm to make a niche for herself in Durban. Going home for a weekend, or for a holiday, was something she always looked forward to, and now she was going home to become engaged to Derek Halstead.

Her parents had approved of him from the start, and during the past eighteen months he had become a regular visitor at Sweet Waters, mainly because he had insisted that the journey was too long and tiresome for Abbey to accomplish on her own. She enjoyed his concern; it made her feel fragile and cared for, and it had been fun showing him all her secret places on the farm where she had played as a child.

Her excitement increased as they drove along the

winding hillside road. Eagle's Peak came into view, and a half hour later they were driving through the white-pillared entrance which led up to the gabled homestead which stood against the backdrop of rugged, towering mountains. The sound of Derek's Mercedes coming up the drive captured the attention of her parents, and they rushed out of the house to welcome them.

'Abbey! Derek!' Claire Mitchell exclaimed, hugging them both in a charming yet detached manner before she stepped back to observe them a little reprovingly. 'We expected you sooner.'

'We unfortunately left a little late,' Abbey explained briefly, stepping away from the slender, well-preserved woman with the black hair which was greying attractively at the temples.

'Where are your parents, Derek?' Claire wanted to know while Abbey turned eagerly into her father's arms.

'They had to collect Dalene at the university, but they should be here within the hour,' Abbey heard Derek explain while she wrapped her arms about her father's waist, and kissed his leathery cheek.

'Hello, Dad,' she smiled up at him.

'Hello, my dear,' Edward Mitchell grinned down at her, his blue eyes filled with a tender warmth, and strands of grey hair falling in a disorderly fashion across his broad forehead as the breeze lifted it. 'Did you have a good trip?'

'It was tiring,' she admitted, conscious of a stiffness in her legs. 'And I could do with something cool to drink.'

The men shook hands affably, and then Derek was carrying their suitcases into the house with its cool, carpeted interior, and the priceless antiques which her parents had collected over the years.

'You know the way to the guest-room, Derek,' her mother was saying, 'and we'll expect you and Abbey in the living-room as soon as you've freshened up.'

Derek nodded, taking Abbey's suitcase to her bedroom before going along to his own and, left alone, Abbey rushed across to the window. Her fingers fumbled impatiently with the catch and, opening it wide, she breathed the fresh country air deep into her lungs like someone who had suppressed a craving far too long.

It was good to be home, she thought, watching a wisp of cloud in the sky which looked as if it were scraping the scraggy tip of Eagle's Peak. They had had good rains at Sweet Waters since the start of spring, and wherever she looked it was as if a green carpet had been spread out across the earth. She could stand there for hours simply staring at the mountains from her window, but her parents were awaiting them in the living-room, and her mother was not, by nature, a patient woman.

Abbey left her room a few minutes later after having changed into a cool, creaseless silk dress with an attractive floral design, but when she passed the guest-room she found Derek standing in front of the window and staring out at the mountains as she had done a while before.

'Your parents have a lovely home, Abbey,' he said, turning at the sound of her light step when she entered his room. 'There's a wonderful view of the mountains from here, and it's one of the things I have always looked forward to.'

'I feel the same way about it,' she said, the warmth of a smile in her eyes as they met his.

'Come here,' he ordered softly.

'Not now, Derek,' she protested when he reached for her, but she did not complain too much when she found herself trapped lightly in his arms. 'My parents are expecting us,' she tried again.

'They can wait a little longer,' he insisted, then his lips were pressed against hers, and they were warm and firm, but without that sensual, sexually arousing quality she had disliked so much in the men she had known before.

Abbey relaxed against him and slipped her arms about his neck so that her fingers could brush lightly against his soft fair hair. His arms tightened about her at once, bringing her closer to the lean length of his body, and the suppressed passion in his kiss stirred the surface of her emotions pleasantly.

'I still can't believe my luck,' he sighed when at last he raised his head to look down into her eyes. 'It took me so long to persuade you to marry me that I'm finding it difficult to believe that you actually agreed.'

She tilted her head in an unconsciously provocative manner as she glanced up at him. 'I needed time to make up my mind about you.'

'And now?'

'I think I've made the right decision,' she replied gravely, but her eyes held a teasing light as she observed the expression on his face.

'You think?' he demanded with a hint of anxiety.

'All right, darling—I know,' she laughed softly, brushing her fingers lightly over his hair in a way which she knew pleased him. 'Does that make you feel happier?'

His eyes darkened. 'I love you, Abbey.'

Her smile did not waver, but inwardly she felt troubled. *I love you*, was something she was not yet able to say, but if Derek was aware of her omission then he did not remark upon it, and it was something she was grateful for.

'My parents will be searching for us in a moment if we don't make a move towards the living-room,' she remonstrated with him, shutting out her disturbing thoughts.

'Ah, well,' Derek sighed, releasing her only to take her hand and pull it through his arm, 'I presume we'd better join them.'

When they entered the spacious living-room a few minutes later Claire and Edward Mitchell gave no indication of the impatience they must have felt, and Edward rose at once from his chair to ask, 'Could I offer you a beer, Derek?'

'That would be nice, thank you,' Derek replied at once, joining her father at the oak cabinet against the wall with its built-in refrigerator.

'I'll help myself to a glass of iced lime juice,' Abbey assured her father when he glanced at her enquiringly over his shoulder, and the ice tinkled in the tall glass when she seated herself beside her mother on the sofa.

'I have everything organised for tomorrow evening, Abbey,' Claire said, her grey eyes glittering with an inner excitement as she went into detail about the arrangements she had made for the following evening when Derek would slip that expensive engagement ring on to Abbey's finger, but Abbey was listening to it all without taking much of it in. She made the required responses, but somehow her ears were straining to catch the drift of the conversation between Derek and her father.

'What was that you were saying, Dad, about an artist on the farm, or something?' she finally interrupted her mother to glance at her father curiously.

'I was telling Derek about the artist who's camping out on our farm,' Edward explained. 'His name is Hammond Scott.'

'Never heard of him,' Abbey frowned, disappointed

when her mind failed to conjure up this man's work. 'What made him want to stop over here at Sweet Waters?'

'The scenery apparently appealed to him, and he asked permission to do a landscape with the house as a focal point,' Edward replied, taking a mouthful of beer and wiping the froth off his upper lip with the back of his hand. 'He seemed a likeable chap, so I agreed.'

'When did he arrive?' Abbey continued to question her father, ignoring the curious glances Derek was directing at her.

'He arrived last Friday, as a matter of fact.'

'How long is he staying?'

'I have no idea,' her father shrugged. 'A month, or maybe two.'

'You're showing a great deal of interest in this artist chap, I must say,' Derek intervened with an odd mixture of humour and suspicion in his dark eyes. 'Are you sure you don't know him?'

'Don't be silly, Derek,' she laughed shortly. 'You know I have this desire to dabble in art occasionally, so naturally I'm interested.'

'He's camping out in his caravan in that sheltered spot across the stream, and he's really no trouble at all,' Claire remarked graciously, joining in the conversation. 'He makes his own meals, and does his own washing.'

'He must be eccentric,' Derek observed at once with all the symptoms of someone looking down his nose at someone else and, sensing the insult behind his statement, Abbey found herself becoming annoyed for some unknown reason.

'How can you say that?' she demanded sharply. 'You don't even know the man.'

'Artists are usually eccentric,' Derek insisted stubbornly, gaining obvious favour from Claire Mitchell.

'Because you know of a few bearded, scruffy artists living in squalor it doesn't necessarily mean that this man falls into the same category,' Abbey found herself arguing heatedly in the defence of a man she had never met.

'I was merely passing a casual remark, Abbey,' he laughed comfortably. 'Don't bite my head off, will you?'

'There's nothing scruffy about Hammond Scott, I can assure you,' her father intervened. 'I had to pass by his caravan yesterday, and for an artist he keeps it exceptionally neat and tidy.'

'There, you see?' Abbey remarked pointedly, glancing at Derek, and it was with the greatest difficulty that she did not revert back to the childish habit of sticking her tongue out at him.

'I'm not arguing with you, darling, and I give in gracefully,' Derek announced laughingly, raising his hands in a gesture of submission, and her inexplicable anger simmered down as quickly as it had risen.

'Any possibility of meeting him, Dad?' she asked, aware of Derek's frowning glance resting on her once more.

'I shouldn't think so,' Edward replied doubtfully. 'He keeps very much to himself, and——'

'I would prefer it if you stayed away from him, Abbey,' her mother interrupted disapprovingly. 'I admit that it's thrilling having an artist here on the farm wanting to paint the ceramic beauty of our home, but he's a stranger to us, and one can never be sure of what kind of man he really is.'

'Oh, for goodness' sake!' Abbey protested, hating her mother's snobbish attitude. 'You're making the man sound quite frightening, and that without the slightest proof.'

'Your mother's right,' her father agreed with obvious reluctance. 'We don't really know the man except for what we've seen, and until we do know him better it would perhaps be advisable if you steered clear of him.'

Abbey opened her mouth to object, but the sound of a car coming up the drive forestalled her.

'This must be your parents, Derek,' Claire announced, rising to her feet.

'If it is, then they've made good time,' Derek smiled, glancing at his watch, and he rose eagerly from his chair to follow Claire from the living-room.

Abbey and her father followed in their wake and reached the door just in time to see the long black limousine slide to a halt behind Derek's Mercedes.

Jeanette and Frank Halstead were the kind of people Abbey's mother thrived on. They had wealth and status, two very important ingredients in Claire Mitchell's opinion, and she welcomed them, as well as their daughter, Dalene, with a regality she reserved for such occasions.

When the sun began to set beyond the mountains like a flaming ball in the sky, Abbey found herself sitting next to Derek in the living-room while she listened to everyone trying to talk at once. The engagement party took priority, naturally, until Abbey felt like asking Derek to take her somewhere quiet where they could become engaged officially without all the unnecessary to-do.

Dalene, fair-haired and dark-eyed like her brother, was the only one, other than Abbey, not taking part in the enthusiastic discussion, and when they had a moment alone together before going to bed that evening, Abbey discovered why.

'You must be terribly excited about tomorrow evening,' Dalene remarked as she followed Abbey into the

kitchen to make coffee for everyone before they all
retired, and there was something strangely cynical in the
tone of Dalene's voice that placed Abbey instantly on
her guard.

'I suppose I am, yes,' she replied warily, switching on
the kettle and setting out the cups on a tray.

'You don't sound very sure.'

'Of course I'm sure,' Abbey protested calmly, not
liking the look in Dalene's eyes very much.

'I told Derek, once, that he was wasting his time, and
that you would never marry him.'

Abbey was shaken by this disclosure, but she hid this
fact behind the smile she directed at the girl who stood
leaning against the kitchen cupboard. 'That proves how
wrong one can be.'

'You're not married yet, you know,' Dalene said
smugly, and Abbey paused in the process of spooning
instant coffee into the cups.

'You haven't liked me right from the start, and I've
often wondered why.' Her steady, questioning glance
held Dalene's. 'Have I ever done anything to you that
you should feel this way?'

Dalene shrugged, and flicked a silky strand of fair
hair away from her face with a careless gesture of her
hand. 'You're just not right for Derek. I can feel it.'

'Don't you think Derek is old enough to decide for
himself whom he wants to marry?'

'My brother is a fool where women are concerned,'
Dalene laughed cynically. 'He's blindly in love with you,
and he imagines that you feel the same way about him,
but you don't, do you.'

Dalene was not questioning her, but stating a fact,
and Abbey was beginning to feel distinctly annoyed. 'I'm
very fond of Derek, and I think that, together, we could
make a success of marriage. If you expected me to be

hovering somewhere up on an ecstatic cloud, then I'm
going to have to disappoint you. I'm a realist, and I prefer
to face the future with both feet firmly on the ground.'

'What you're really saying is that you don't believe in
love, and all that romantic nonsense.'

'Don't put words into my mouth,' Abbey rebuked
her sharply.

'But it's true, isn't it?'

'I believe in going into marriage with my eyes wide
open, instead of allowing myself to be blinded by false,
unstable emotions,' Abbey replied coolly. 'I know what
I'm doing, and so does Derek.'

'Well, all I can say is, for your sakes, I hope that you
do.'

Dalene smiled twistedly, then she sauntered out of
the kitchen to rejoin the others, leaving a rather bewildered and oddly edgy Abbey alone with her
thoughts.

That night, when she lay awake in the darkness of
her bedroom, her conversation with Dalene kept recur-
ring annoyingly. *Love!* What was love? It was a rather
vague emotion which no one seemed capable of explaining in detail. Desire? Yes, that was an emotion
which she could understand to a certain extent, but it
was not something she liked to dwell on. The word
'desire' had a sexual ring to it, and surely no marriage
could last if it were based on desire alone. Could it?

'Absolutely not!' she answered her own question, her
voice a mere whisper in the darkness. What she and
Derek had was something much more stable than that.
They had each other's respect, they enjoyed each other's
company, and they shared many similar interests.
Granted, there was no ringing of bells in her ears when
they kissed and embraced, but there was instead a
warmth and a quiet happiness at being close to him.

Who wanted the sound of bells in their ears, after all, to disturb their peaceful togetherness?

Love? Well, of course she loved him! Was love not wanting to share the rest of one's life with someone? Naturally she loved Derek! She longed to be with him when they were apart, and she missed him dreadfully when he had to go away on business for a few days. They spoke the same language, literally and figuratively, and, most important of all, neither of them were endowed with extremely passionate natures. Oh, they would have their arguments, as they always did, but life with Derek would be mostly like sailing across calm seas, and that was why she was marrying him.

The Mitchell household was a hive of activity on the Saturday morning when Abbey stepped out on to the terrace and found Derek lounging in a cane chair with an out-of-date magazine.

'Let's go for a walk,' she suggested, wanting to put as much distance as possible between the house and herself, for a while at least.

'Must we?' Derek groaned reluctantly.

'Don't be so lazy,' she laughed down into his eyes. 'It's a beautiful day, and it's peaceful out there.'

The sound of raised voices, and the clattering of crockery being stacked in piles suddenly spilled out on to the terrace as if to emphasise her statement. Derek grimaced as he dropped the magazine on to the table beside him and, placing his hands on the arms of the chair, he levered himself on to his feet.

'You're right about it being peaceful out there,' he said, linking his arm through hers as they walked down the steps and crossed the dew-wet lawn which lay like a sparkling carpet at their feet in the early morning sun. 'Where shall we walk to?'

'Does it matter?'

'I don't actually mind where we go. The important thing is that you're with me,' he smiled down at her, and her heart warmed towards him in that familiar way.

'That's sweet of you, Derek.'

Standing on her toes, she drew his head down and kissed him impulsively on the lips. She had intended it to be a brief kiss, but his arms encircled her waist, and the kiss lengthened pleasantly.

Quite a few seconds elapsed before they continued their walk, and Abbey took Derek in a wide circle which would eventually lead back to the house, but she was in no hurry to get there at all. The air was beautifully clean and fresh, and the birds were chirping lustily in the trees. She missed the birds when she was in Durban, but the pleasure of listening to the birdsong when she returned to Sweet Waters was something special. Cattle grazed lazily in the fields, their presence adding to the tranquillity of the scene, and the familiar smell of the damp earth quivered in her nostrils. It was good to get away from the concrete and steel of the city, from the noise and the pollution, and the endless rush to nowhere in particular, and she took several deep breaths of the sweet, fresh air, wishing almost that she never had to leave the farm again.

Abbey wondered sometimes how Derek felt about spending time on the farm. Being born and bred in the city, she realised that he could not, perhaps, enjoy it to the extent that she did, but whenever he had accompanied her home at weekends he had appeared to relax and enjoy the things which pleased her. He drew the line, though, at mounting a horse. He had been thrown once, and it had been enough to make him lose his nerve. He loved horses, but he remained an admirer with his feet firmly on the ground instead of in the stirrup.

'Couldn't we sit down somewhere?' he complained when they had reached the top of a hill and stood looking down into the valley below.

'We could sit over there,' she said, pointing to a large, flat rock a little distance from them, and as they strolled towards it she laughed up at him teasingly. 'You get too little exercise sitting behind that desk of yours all day.'

'Not everybody is mad enough to go jogging on the beach at sunrise each morning,' he panted, lowering himself on to the rock and stretching his long legs out before him. 'I just don't know how you can do it, and then still put in a whole day at the office.'

Abbey's laughter rang out clearly across the veld. 'You should try it some time. It's invigorating, and fills me with tons of energy for the day.'

'Don't talk about energy,' he groaned, taking his handkerchief out of his pocket and mopping the perspiration from his forehead and neck. 'I think I've done enough walking this morning to last me a lifetime.'

'Oh, well, we're not too far from the house now. We'll rest a while, then we'll go farther.'

'I can't wait for this evening,' Derek said eventually. 'Your ring has been burning a hole in my pocket for the last few days, and I'm longing to put it on your finger to show the whole world that you're promised to me.'

'I'm looking forward to it as well,' she whispered, slipping her hand into his, and loving the way his fingers tightened about hers.

'I love you, Abbey.'

She watched him raise her hand to his lips, and felt again that stab of guilt. Why couldn't she say 'I love you, Derek' as easily as he said 'I love you, Abbey'? What was the matter with her? Why did the words always lodge in her throat like a piece of sticky gum?

'Abbey?' His finger traced her winged eyebrows lazily before travelling down the perfect curve of her cheek to her lips. 'What were you thinking just then?'

'I was thinking . . .' She stopped, startled at the realisation that she had so very nearly voiced her thoughts, and she ended lamely with, 'I was thinking about us.' There was some truth in that, she consoled herself. 'I think we're going to be very happy together.'

'Of course we are,' he smiled, then his arms were about her, and he was kissing her with a warmth that drove her uncomfortable thoughts temporarily from her mind.

It was silly, after all, to worry about something like that. In time she would find it easier to say the words which she knew he must be longing to hear . . . but only in time.

She disengaged herself from his arms after a while, and they continued their walk back to the house in a companionable silence. She felt happy and contented once more, and she actually found herself looking forward to this special evening which she and Derek would have to share with the hordes of guests her mother had invited.

At the bottom end of the garden, some distance from the house, they encountered a man seated on a low canvas stool, and Abbey stared at him frowningly for several seconds before she noticed the sketch pad on his knee.

'Of course! The artist!' she almost said aloud to herself. She had forgotten about him completely, she realised as they paused a little distance from him.

Dressed in nothing but faded denims and leather sandals, he sat with his back towards them, and Abbey had a clear vision of the tanned width of shoulders which tapered down to slim hips. His skin was gleaming in the sunlight, the muscles rippling beneath its smoothness at the slightest movement, but it was his hair that held her attention. It was the most unusual colour, she decided. Short, thick, and neatly trimmed in his strong neck, it had the appearance of burnished copper, and she suddenly had the most unusual desire to know the colour of his eyes.

A twig snapped beneath her foot when they had overcome their surprise sufficiently to approach him, and he looked up at once, casting a glance over his shoulder. A multitude of thoughts and feelings flashed through her at that moment, and Abbey could never recall afterwards what had been her first impression of Hammond Scott. His features were rugged and tanned, and there was just the slightest suggestion of a dent in the square jaw, while the high-bridged nose showed signs of having been broken at some time in his life. There was a hint of cynicism and cruelty in the chiselled mouth despite the sensuous curve of the lower lip, she decided, but it was his eyes beneath the heavy dark brows that caught and held her attention when they were but a few paces from him. They were a mixture of grey and green, and strangely compelling as they surveyed her intently until she felt herself squirming inwardly. Determined to withstand the onslaught of his eyes, she saw them flick over her critically, and she had the strangest feeling that she had been weighed and found wanting.

Hammond Scott was a most peculiar man, she decided at length. Outwardly he appeared calm and unperturbed, but she somehow sensed the energy which lay charged and stored beneath the surface of his exterior. She sensed, too, an awareness within herself; an alertness, perhaps, as if she had come into contact with a force far stronger than her own, but, being a realist, she promptly ignored this.

CHAPTER TWO

'MR SCOTT?' Abbey queried, breaking the awkward silence, and when he nodded without speaking, she said: 'I'm Abbey Mitchell, and this is Derek Halstead.' He gave Derek no more than a cursory glance before returning his attention to her. 'Would it annoy you if we watched you work for a while?' she asked hurriedly, and selfconsciously when an awkward silence threatened once again.

'Please yourself,' he shrugged, and his voice, although abrupt, was deep and pleasant on the ears.

'It's customary, you know, to stand up when a lady speaks to you,' Derek spoke for the first time, and his voice was coldly reproving.

Hammond Scott did not leap to his feet as a lesser man might have done at the authoritative tone of Derek's voice. He remained seated, and his derisive glance took in briefly Abbey's embarrassment before settling intently on Derek. 'I never asked her to speak to me.'

Abbey felt Derek stiffen beside her. 'Why, you——'

'Derek, no!' she intervened swiftly, more concerned for Derek's safety at that moment when she glimpsed the tensing of Hammond Scott's broad shoulders and muscled biceps in preparation for a physical counter-attack. 'Mr Scott is right. He never invited conversation, and neither was it my intention to disturb him in his work,' she announced pacifyingly with a restraining hand on Derek's arm, then she glanced at the man seated on the low stool and added: 'Please, do go on as if we weren't here.'

'With pleasure,' he said abruptly, his mouth twisting into what could be termed as a smile, but it did not reach his eyes.

Abbey sensed that Derek was bristling with angry impatience, but she chose to ignore it as she leaned closer to glance over one of Hammond Scott's broad shoulders at the charcoal pencil making decisive strokes across the sheet of paper. He was sketching the house against the backdrop of the mountains, and he could not have chosen a better day on which to do so. Dragon's Cove, rugged and beautiful, stood etched against the clear blue sky, and nestled at the foot of it was the gabled homestead with its gleaming white walls and sparkling windows. It was surrounded by shady trees and a sloping lawn, and all this Hammond Scott had managed to capture in detail.

'As a preliminary sketch, that's really excellent,' she could not prevent herself from saying, and his strong, long-fingered hand stilled its action.

'Do you think so?' he asked without looking up at her, and the mockery in his voice sent a rush of colour into her cheeks, but she nevertheless persisted in questioning him, her interest genuine.

'Do you always make an initial sketch, or do you sometimes put the object you're painting directly on to canvas?'

'That depends on what I'm doing, and where I happen to be.' He looked up unexpectedly, and the mockery she had heard in his voice was there in his eyes when they met hers. 'Right here and now it wouldn't pay to put my ideas directly on to canvas. Of all the sketches I shall eventually select only a few which I shall reproduce on canvas.'

'We should be going, Abbey,' Derek intervened, standing about restlessly.

'In just a minute,' she said quickly, casting Derek an appealing glance before returning her attention to Hammond Scott. 'Do you do this for a living?'

A gleam of sardonic amusement flashed in his eyes. 'You could say so, yes.'

'No one could possibly make a decent living out of this sort of thing,' Derek announced in a disparaging voice that made her cast a reproving glance in his direction. 'Artists are generally a lazy lot, living on dreams of wealth, instead of working for a living like everyone else.'

'Derek!' she exclaimed in a shocked voice, annoyed by his tactless remark.

'You obviously have a low opinion of artists, Mr Halstead, but they work equally hard to capture on canvas what others take for granted,' Hammond Scott replied in a totally unperturbed manner, but his unusual eyes were now more green than grey, and Abbey glimpsed a flash of derisive anger in their depths. 'This type of work does allow us a certain amount of freedom even though it doesn't bring in much money, but if no one succumbed to the urge to put their artistic talents to use, *you* wouldn't be able to walk through the art galleries with your wealthy friends in order to impress them with your knowledge of the arts—if you have any knowledge of it, that is.'

Hammond Scott had put Derek very smartly in his place, Abbey thought, and she felt a little ashamed at the flicker of admiration she felt for this man, but she had no time to dwell on it, for Derek was advancing on Hammond with his fists raised and clenched.

'If you think I'll take your insults lightly, then——'

'Derek, please!' Abbey stopped him, her fingers tightening over the tensed muscles in his forearm when she glimpsed once again the flexing of those bulging muscles on Hammond Scott's chest and arms. He had the appearance of a man quite capable in the art of self-defence, and she had an alarming suspicion that he was simply aching for the opportunity to ram one of those large fists into Derek's handsome face. 'You were rather insulting in your own way, you know,' she reminded Derek in a pacifying, but reproving voice.

'Are you choosing to side with this ne'er-do-well instead of with me?' Derek demanded furiously.

'It's not a matter of choosing sides, Derek, but be fair,' she pleaded softly. 'You did rather insult Mr Scott.'

'What I said was the truth,' Derek persisted with a doggedness which was not entirely unfamiliar to her. 'Artists are generally a lazy lot.'

Angered by his attitude, she said a trifle sharply, 'In your opinion, perhaps, but then you're a born nine-to-five man with no ambition in any other direction.'

'Abbey!'

He looked shocked and hurt, and she felt miserable knowing that she was the cause of it, but she could not allow him to insult this man in the way he had done without making her displeasure known.

'Oh, let's drop the subject,' she sighed.

'I'd be grateful if the two of you would continue your argument somewhere else,' Hammond Scott remarked drily, and a wave of guilt swept over Abbey as she turned to face him.

'I'm sorry,' she said apologetically, unable to meet his eyes.

'Come along, Abbey,' Derek instructed, taking her arm in a firm grip and literally dragging her away.

'Just a minute,' she protested, pulling her arm free of his clasp and glancing back at the man seated on the

canvas stool who was obviously observing them with
some amusement. She was not quite sure what she had
intended to say, but she felt somehow responsible for
Derek's wounding remarks, and the words that finally
tumbled from her lips were, 'Are you doing anything
special this evening, Mr Scott?'

Those heavy eyebrows rose a fraction. 'Not that I can
recall.'

'Derek and I are getting engaged this evening, and it's
going to be quite a party,' she rushed on heedlessly.
'Would you care to come along?'

Mild surprise was mirrored fractionally in his eyes
before he flicked a glance at the immaculately dressed
man beside her, then a faintly mocking smile curved his
mouth. 'I'm afraid I don't have an evening suit handy.'

'Please feel free to wear whatever you wish,' Abbey
replied generously, thinking that the poor man probably
did not even possess such a thing as an evening suit.
'May we expect you?'

'I'd be delighted.'

'See you at seven-thirty, then,' she smiled briefly.

'Are you crazy, inviting a man like that to our engagement party?' Derek demanded angrily as they
walked away.

'Keep your voice down, Derek!' Abbey hissed at him,
adding defiantly, 'And I shall invite whom I please.'

Derek's dark eyes looked stormy. 'I shudder to think
what our parents are going to have to say about this.'

'I couldn't care less *what* they have to say about it,'
she retorted angrily. 'Not one of the hundred guests
expected here this evening were invited by me, and I,
after all, have the right to invite someone of my own
choice.'

'But, Abbey, this artist fellow is not in our class at
all.'

'Who says he's not?' she demanded fiercely, discovering for the first time that Derek had a distasteful tendency towards snobbery. 'Besides, what does it matter?' she added sharply.

'I simply don't understand you when you're like this,' he said when they paused at the steps leading up on to the terrace.

'Then we're even, Derek, because I can't understand why you had to be so damned nasty to the man.'

'I was merely——'

'Stating your opinion, yes,' she finished for him irritably. 'But don't you ever stop to consider that your opinions might be viewed as an insult from someone else's point of view?'

Derek's jaw set with a familiar determination which she now recognised as stubbornness. 'But I've never yet met an artist who's been able to make a living out of painting silly little pictures, and I don't see why——'

'Oh, shut up, Derek!' she exclaimed exasperatedly. 'There are times when you make me feel quite sick!'

Turning on her heel, she raced up the steps and into the house. It had to be Dalene, of all people, with whom she collided in the hall, and judging by the oddly triumphant expression on her face, she had heard Abbey's last remark. With a muttered apology, Abbey brushed past her, quickening her pace when she reached the passage, and when she stormed into her bedroom she slammed the door behind her with an unnecessary force.

'To the devil with Dalene! To the devil with everyone!' she muttered furiously, falling across her bed, and then, to her horror, she burst into tears.

An hour later, her anger forgotten and feeling decidedly better after having a good cry, she emerged from her room and went in search of Derek. She found him on the terrace, smoking a cigarette and staring moodily out across the garden, but at the sound of her step behind him he turned, and flicked his half-smoked cigarette over the low wall.

'I'm sorry, Abbey,' he said, remorse in his eyes as he grasped her outstretched hands. 'I never intended to make you angry.'

'Don't apologise,' she smiled a little guiltily. 'I guess I must have the jitters about tonight, that's all.'

'Oh, Abbey . . .'

He drew her into his arms, but, before his lips could touch hers, Dalene's cynical voice made them draw apart hastily.

'Am I intruding?'

'Yes, you are,' Derek informed his sister with frowning displeasure.

'Sorry,' she shrugged carelessly. 'The folks want you both in the living-room to discuss this evening's proceedings.'

Derek sighed audibly, and Abbey echoed that sigh inwardly as they entered the house hand in hand with Dalene leading the way with a self-satisfied look on her face. Abbey could imagine what she was thinking. She could imagine what she was hoping for, too, but right this minute she did not want to think about it. Dalene's attitude merely annoyed her, and she did not want to be annoyed once again that morning.

Somehow, during the course of the day, neither Abbey, nor Derek found the opportunity to mention her impulsive invitation to Hammond Scott, and that evening, with the glittering impressive dining-hall crowded with people who were spilling out on to the terrace, Abbey decided that it had perhaps been wiser to remain siilent. It was almost eight o'clock, and Hammond Scott's absence made her suspect that he had changed his mind about coming after all. She felt strangely disappointed, but as she walked at Derek's side, mingling politely with their guests, she soon forgot about him.

Abbey happened to be standing next to her mother some minutes later when she heard Claire draw her breath in sharply, and following the direction of her mother's gaze, she saw Hammond Scott lounging against one of the doors leading out on to the terrace. Dressed in an open-necked shirt, blue denim jacket and pants, and canvas shoes, he looked so blessedly casual and relaxed among all the stiff formality that Abbey felt some of the tension ease away from her as if he had offered her a much-needed antidote.

'What on earth is that man doing here? And look at the way he's dressed!' Claire exploded with indignation, then she turned to her husband and demanded sharply, 'Did you invite him, Edward?'

'I wouldn't have invited him without your knowledge, Claire,' he replied with a puzzled frown on his brow.

'Well then, who——'

'I invited him, Mother,' Abbey interrupted quietly.

'*You?*' Her mother turned on her like a ferocious cat with its eyes narrowed and teeth bared. 'But what on earth possessed you to do such a thing?'

'Does it matter?'

'Of course it matters!' Claire swung round to her husband and gestured imperiously. 'Edward, you must order him to leave at once!'

'You'll do no such thing!' Abbey intervened with a stamp of determination on her lovely face which her mother had never seen before. 'Hammond Scott is my guest, and he'll leave only when he decides to do so.'

'Well, really! I——'

Abbey did not stay to hear more, and made her way

quickly among the guests to where Hammond stood observing the proceedings idly with an amber-coloured drink in his hand. Abbey was aware of the whispered comments doing the rounds, and so was Hammond, judging by the gleam of sardonic humour in his eyes.

'Hello,' she smiled when she reached his side, and she discovered to her surprise that he was a great deal taller than she had imagined he would be. He was, in fact, several inches taller than Derek, she realised as she tilted her head back to say, 'I was beginning to think you'd changed your mind about coming.'

'I was delayed in town this afternoon.' His grey-green glance slid over her, taking in the peach-coloured silk of her dress where it clung softly to the gentle curves of her figure, and there was an odd fluttering in her throat when his eyes met hers once more. 'That's a stunning dress you're wearing, by the way.'

'Thank you,' she managed awkwardly, aware of her femininity in a way she had never been before, and she lowered her eyes hastily, not quite sure how to deal with it.

'Am I an embarrassment to you, putting in an appearance dressed like this?' he asked unexpectedly, making her realise once again that he was not unaware of the whispered and unflattering comments his presence was arousing. 'Would you prefer it if I left, Miss Mitchell?'

'Don't be silly!' she snapped, a part of her mind registering the fact that his hair had adopted a dark brown colour in the artificial light. 'I told you to wear whatever you wished—and my name, by the way, is Abbey.'

'Short for Abigail?' he asked at once, a faintly mocking light in his eyes as they dwelled on the smooth contours of her face with the keen intensity of an artist studying his subject.

'Yes,' she grimaced. There was a strained little silence, but when she noticed that his glass was empty, she asked: 'Could I get you something to drink, or perhaps you'd like something to eat?'

'I'll help myself later,' he declined, then he glanced at her hand which was still devoid of any adornment. 'I'm still in time to witness the engagement, it seems.'

'Mother has decided that nine o'clock would be the best time for the announcement to be made. Everyone would still be sober enough at that time to know what's going on.'

'A wise decision,' he grinned twistedly, watching a tray of drinks being emptied with the swiftness of an eagle swooping down on its prey. The dining-hall was crowded with men dressed in impeccably tailored evening suits, and women displaying their expensive array of jewels. Abbey stared at them for a while, then she became conscious of Hammond watching her closely. 'Do you know all these people here this evening?' he asked casually.

'Not all of them,' she laughed softly, ignoring the curious glances directed at them as she took in the formidable width of his shoulders beneath the denim jacket. 'They're mostly farmers in the district, or business associates of my father's from Pietermaritzburg, but the Halsteads have invited quite a number of their own family and friends whom I haven't met as yet.'

'Who's the blonde girl who seems to be giving us such disapproving looks?'

Very carefully, Abbey allowed her glance to follow the direction of his, and her stomach twisted once again into a hard knot. 'That's Dalene, Derek's sister. I'm afraid she doesn't like me very much.'

Hammond's mouth twisted cynically. 'Perhaps she doesn't like the idea that you're seen associating with me.'

'She's a snob,' Abbey grimaced.

'Aren't most people?'

'I would like to think that I'm not.' She turned her back on glaring dark eyes, and looked a long way up into Hammond Scott's tanned, rugged face. 'How long are you staying here on the farm?'

'That depends,' he shrugged, placing his empty glass on a tray as one of the white-coated servants passed them.

'Depends on what?' she demanded curiously.

'I'll pack up and leave when I have enough sketches to take home with me.'

'Where's home?' His expression became oddly shuttered, and she heard herself asking quickly, 'Do you find my curiosity annoying?'

'Not at all,' he said at length, a hint of mockery in his eyes. 'My home is in Johannesburg.'

A couple brushed past them, passing loud remarks about the way Hammond was dressed. It was intentional, she knew that, and her blue eyes sparkled with suppressed fury when she saw the tight-lipped cynicism hovering about Hammond's mouth.

'Don't pay any attention to what they're saying,' she said, her hand gripping his arm and coming into contact with the tautness of his muscles through the denim material of his jacket. 'I'm very glad you came.'

'Are you?'

'I'm not in the habit of saying things I don't mean.'

'That's not quite the truth, is it?' The muscles in his arm relaxed fractionally, but his expression remained unaltered. 'You never actually intended inviting me this morning, but you'd been somewhat inconvenienced by your fiancé's remarks, and anything would have sufficed at the time. Unfortunately, you chose to invite me here this evening.'

'Why unfortunately?' she asked warily, removing her hand from his arm and marvelling at the fact that he had been so shrewd in his assumption.

'I accepted, didn't I?' he enlightened her mockingly. 'And now *I'm* the one who's an embarrassment to you, although you're trying very hard not to show it.'

'That's not true!' she protested at once. 'I admit that I was embarrassed this morning, and I admit that my invitation was issued impulsively, but I'm not ashamed or embarrassed in any way by your presence, and if you think that, then I——'

'Then you what?' he prompted when she paused abruptly.

Essentially an honest person, Abbey answered him truthfully, but not without a certain amount of discomfiture. 'I was going to say, then I wouldn't waste another minute on you, but that would have been childish, and silly.'

His eyes narrowed. 'In what way?'

'Because this disgustingly formal affair was boring me to tears until the moment I saw you standing here.'

Out of the corner of her eye she glimpsed her mother's outraged expression and that of the Halsteads, but at that moment she was more concerned with the man before her, and the gleam of mockery which leapt so unexpectedly into his eyes.

'I hope your fiancé isn't a jealous man, Abbey, or that remark might give him the wrong idea.'

A wave of colour surged into her cheeks, but her gaze did not falter. 'You understood what I meant by it, though, didn't you?'

'I'd be a fool if I didn't,' he said abruptly, and she was surprised to see anger lurking with equal suddenness in those eyes which held her glance so compellingly.

'You're using me to thumb your nose at all your stuffy friends, and I think it's time I put an end to it.'

'Hammond ... don't go,' she pleaded, her hand gripping his arm when he would have turned to leave. 'You're the only friend I have here this evening,' she confided, and she realised, somewhat to her surprise, that this was the truth.

'Your "poor little rich girl" act doesn't impress me, Miss Mitchell,' he replied with a cynicism that made her wince inwardly as it sliced right through her.

'Please . . .' she begged desperately, her hand tightening on his arm when he tried to draw it from her clasp. 'I very much want you to stay, and you're wrong if you think I'm using you in the disgusting way you mentioned.'

He studied her for a moment, his jaw hard and unrelenting as he took in her wide, anxious eyes, the unnatural paleness in her cheeks, and the quivering of her soft, generous mouth. Abbey held her breath, her nails digging unconsciously into the denim of his jacket, then his expression relaxed slightly. 'I believe you really mean that.'

'I do,' she confessed in an urgent whisper. 'I honestly do!'

His eyes held hers captive for interminable seconds during which everyone and everything seemed to fade away strangely, leaving only the two of them, and she felt again that odd fluttering in her throat.

'Excuse me for interrupting this tender little scene,' Dalene's sarcastic voice intervened, and Abbey's hand fell away from Hammond's arm as they turned to face her. 'Someone ought to remind you, Abbey, that you have other, more important guests to see to,' Dalene stated cuttingly, and her haughty glance indicated clearly that she considered Hammond's status on a par with the garbage removal gang in the city.

'Thank you, Dalene, but the importance of our guests can't be measured on a scale, and I would never dream of insulting anyone by attempting to do so,' Abbey replied coldly, and with a matching sarcasm.

'Abbey!' Derek's voice reached her ears moments before he appeared at her side and, rudely ignoring Hammond's presence, he placed a possessive hand on her arm. 'I've been looking everywhere for you.'

'Have you?' she asked, not particularly caring as her anxious glance took in the brittle harshness of Hammond's expression.

'I really think you have a nerve, Mr Whoever-you-are, coming here in that atrociously common outfit,' Dalene attacked Hammond openly, and Abbey could willingly have struck her.

'The name is Scott. Hammond Scott,' he replied with a derisive twist to his mouth as he looked the twenty-year-old Dalene up and down. 'And I'm here at Miss Mitchell's invitation.'

'She *would* invite you,' Dalene snapped vindictively. 'I've known all along that she would give anything to disrupt the arrangements for this evening, and she's certainly succeeded.'

'Dalene, that's not true!' Abbey protested fiercely.

'Isn't it?' Dalene's smile was venomous. 'Well, you've certainly given that impression.'

'Come with me, Abbey,' Derek instructed before she could defend herself. 'There's someone I'd like you to meet.'

Derek's hand urged her away from Hammond, but she stood firm and cast a pleading glance in Hammond's direction. 'I'll have to go, but—we'll talk again later.'

Hammond's eyes were like chips of ice when they met hers, and a coldness seemed to invade her body, then he nodded abruptly, and walked towards the table where the drinks were laid out.

'Did you have to cause such a disturbance among the guests by talking to that artist fellow?' Derek demanded in a reproving whisper as he guided her among the people towards the other end of the room.

'He has a name, Derek,' she said curtly, realising dismally that Dalene had certainly won this round. 'It's Hammond Scott, remember?'

'Let's not argue, darling,' he brushed aside her remark. 'I'd like you to meet a few very old friends of the family.'

Abbey was not in the mood for meeting strangers; not at that precise moment while she was trying so desperately to control the inexplicable anger that raged within her. Dalene had had no right to make those vile, untruthful statements, and neither did she have the right to behave in such a disgustingly superior fashion towards Hammond Scott. It made Abbey cringe inwardly when she thought of it, and it intensified her anger to think that Derek had actually allowed his sister to insult Hammond in that unnecessary way.

She was too distressed after what had occurred to register the names of the two elderly couples Derek had introduced her to, but she somehow managed to talk to them without them suspecting the turmoil her mind was in. It was fortunate, however, that they did not have to prolong their conversation, for Claire was gesturing them towards the small dais her father had erected. It was time to announce their engagement.

This was the moment she had looked forward to, but somehow there was no happiness in the thought, only an uneasy feeling that something was terribly wrong. This was ridiculous! she argued with herself. She was becoming engaged to Derek, and it was something they had planned and discussed for quite some time. Tall, fair and attractive, Derek took her hand and escorted her towards the dais. She smiled up at him, trying desperately to recapture some of her earlier happiness and contentment, but she failed when her glance travelled across the room towards the man who leaned nonchalantly against one of the doors leading out on to the terrace. Hammond Scott was observing the proceedings intently, and when their eyes met across the crowded room her uneasiness returned sharply.

'Ladies and gentlemen, may I have your attention, please?' Edward Mitchell spoke in a raised voice, and the laughter and the conversation ended abruptly. 'It gives me great pleasure to announce the engagement of our daughter, Abbey, to Derek Halstead. Will you all please fill your glasses?' There was a scuffle for a few seconds as everyone made a grab for a glass of champagne, and then there was silence once again. 'To Abbey and Derek,' her father announced, and while everyone drank a toast to their happiness, Derek slid the elaborate engagement ring on to Abbey's finger.

She was conscious of several things at once; of the love in Derek's eyes, the smiles of satisfaction that passed between their respective parents, Dalene's mask-like features, and the cynical, faintly amused smile that curved Hammond Scott's mouth. It was the latter which caused her the most concern for some reason, and when Derek's lips brushed hers, she could almost sense Hammond's cynical smile deepening.

What happened afterwards was a bit of a nightmare with everyone surging forward to offer their congratulations personally, and it was with an extraordinary feeling of relief that she turned eventually to see Hammond approaching them.

'May I offer my congratulations?' he said in a clipped

voice, extending a hand towards Derek, but, when it was rudely ignored, he smiled twistedly and let it fall to his side.

'I thought you would have had the decency to leave by now, Scott.'

Abbey drew a sharp, angry breath. 'That was uncalled for, Derek!'

He scowled at Hammond, then turned away, giving his attention to someone else, and the look on Hammond's face told Abbey that he despised people like Derek, but there was also a look of secret amusement which puzzled her momentarily.

Hammond took her hand in his, and the touch of those strong fingers sent odd little tremors up the length of her arm. He smiled a peculiar smile as he stared down at her engagement ring, then he said bluntly, 'If this is what you want, Abbey, then I wish you well.'

He turned on his heel and shouldered his way out among the people still milling around to speak to them, and she wondered confusedly what he had meant by that remark. 'If this is what you want, then I wish you well.'

Someone else demanded her attention at that moment, and she shelved her thoughts temporarily to concentrate on the people around them, but when the excitement finally died down, Abbey's eyes searched the room for Hammond Scott. He was nowhere in sight, and, as the evening wore on laboriously, she realised that he must have left soon after offering her his congratulations. She felt disappointed, and strangely hurt, but she forcibly shrugged off this feeling.

When at last everyone had departed from Sweet Waters that night, Abbey stared around her at the shambles left by the guests, and she sighed tiredly. Frank and Jeanette Halstead seemed delighted at the success of the evening, and so also Abbey's parents, but Dalene had to voice her displeasure at Hammond Scott being invited. This, of course, triggered everyone else off, and for several minutes Abbey silently endured the barrage of disapproval directed at her from all sides. Derek himself had quite a lot to say about Hammond, and it would have angered Abbey had she not been so tired.

'I'm sorry, Abbey,' Derek said eventually when everyone else had gone to bed and they were alone. 'I just can't stand the fellow.'

'I wish I could understand why.'

Derek shrugged and smiled crookedly. 'Perhaps I'm just a little bit jealous of the interest you've shown in him.'

'Oh, really, Derek!' she exclaimed with a doubtful laugh. 'There's no earthly reason for you to be jealous, and you know it.'

'Sorry, darling, but you don't realise how lovely you are, and no full-blooded male could look at you and not feel something stirring in his breast.'

Abbey stared up at him in shocked surprise, then she lightened the tension by saying teasingly, 'You sound quite poetic!'

'It's the truth,' Derek insisted, and then he was taking her into his arms and kissing her with a tender passion. 'The party was quite a success, don't you think?'

'When you take everything into consideration, then I suppose it was,' she sighed, leaning against him comfortably, and rubbing her cheek against the roughness of his jacket.

'Tired?'

'Yes,' she nodded, not wanting to enter into a lengthy discussion, but admitting to herself that she was more confused than tired at that moment. 'I think I'd like to go to my room.'

'Very well, darling,' he smiled at her with unmistakable pride in his eyes and, outside her bedroom door moments later, he kissed her lingeringly on the lips. 'See you in the morning.'

Abbey did not go to bed at once, but sat for a long time staring at the unfamiliar and ostentatious diamond glittering harshly on her finger. They had chosen it together, or perhaps it would be more truthful to say that Derek had made up her mind for her. She would have preferred something smaller and less conspicuous, but Derek had wanted the largest diamond possible. It felt heavy on her finger, and suddenly it simply added to the list of incidents which had appeared so absolutely wrong that evening.

She went to bed, but, despite her tiredness, she could not sleep. She was besieged with doubts in a way she had never been before. She had looked forward to this weekend; to becoming engaged to Derek. Why, suddenly, did it all seem so wrong? Was it perhaps the discovery that Derek, too, was a status-conscious snob, as well as stubborn in his efforts to cling to his distorted views? She was beginning to suspect that it was, but then she could see no reason why it should matter. If she cared for him as much as she believed she did, then this was something which they should be able to overcome together. Surely, in time, he would unbend a little in that direction to see things her way?

Abbey was suddenly not so sure about that, and she stared doubtfully into the silent darkness until she finally went to sleep.

CHAPTER THREE

DRESSED in comfortable brown slacks, a pale lemon blouse, and riding boots, Abbey left the house at the first light of dawn the following morning, and walked briskly towards the stables. With the help of Barney, the young stable boy, she saddled Nomad, the black Arab stallion which had been a gift from her father two years ago. The animal was restless, the muscles rippling beneath its gleaming coat as if to make her aware of the fact that he had waited long for this wild gallop across the veld which she contemplated.

'Easy, Nomad, easy,' she spoke soothingly, and Nomad pricked back his ears and snorted with a measure of impatience as she led him from the stable.

In one swift, agile movement she was seated in the saddle, and Nomad, temperamental as always after a long absence of having her familiar weight on his back, reared and clawed the air with his front legs, but Abbey remained in the saddle, controlling him with the expertise of one who had spent many hours on horseback.

Barney, his black eyes like saucers in his brown face whenever he witnessed this scene, leapt back several paces, and then he was shaking his head as horse and rider thundered across the yard towards the gate. Nomad did not hesitate, and took the gate like a practiced show jumper, then they were careering across the veld as if a desert storm itself was closing in on them.

Abbey felt exhilarated. The wind was whistling past her ears, and her hair, released from its confining knot, streamed out behind her. With the smell of horseflesh

and leather in her nostrils, she could almost forget her
cares, but not altogether. Fifteen minutes later, their
wild chase at an end, Nomad pawed the ground restlessly, but Abbey's hands were firm on the reins while
she watched the sun rise in the east to spread its golden
glow over the dewy earth. She had watched the sun rise
many times before, but on each occasion it was like a
new experience as she heard and saw the earth come
alive.

She urged the agitated Nomad into a slow canter,
and the sound of his approaching hooves sent a half
dozen pheasants scattering with loud cries from the
acacia tree where they had roosted for the night.

Through the trees, on the opposite side of the stream,
she glimpsed an unfamiliar sight. A caravan, with its
rally tent pitched for shade and comfort, stood on a
level piece of ground, and a battered-looking jeep had
been parked next to it. This was, of course, where
Hammond Scott was camping out, and she instinctively
reined in her horse, not wanting to intrude on his privacy, but she yielded to the temptation and decided to
pay him a visit when she saw Hammond moving about
outside the caravan.

Her cheeks had been stung a delicate pink by the
breeze during her early morning dash across the veld,
and her blue eyes sparkled in the aftermath of enjoyment
as she crossed the low bridge spanning the water and
approached the caravan. Her dark hair hung in wild,
soft curls down her back, and, slim and supple like a
young twig, her body moved in perfect unison with the
animal beneath her. Hammond turned from his task of
lighting the gas fire as she reined in her horse at a nearby
tree, and even from a distance she was aware of the
hostile narrowing of his eyes.

He was wearing the same faded denims and sandals

he had worn the day before, but on this occasion he was also wearing a red checked shirt which was unbuttoned and hanging free of his belt, and there was an aura of unmistakable masculinity about him now that made her draw her breath in sharply. His hair, once again the colour of burnished copper in the slanted rays of the early morning sun, lay untidily across his broad forehead as if he had used his fingers instead of a comb, and his wide, deeply tanned chest was covered in short, dark hair which trailed a path down to his navel.

'You left early last night,' she accused, sliding off Nomad's back and tethering him to the tree.

'Yes,' was all Hammond said.

'Why?' she asked bluntly, walking towards the small fold-up table where he stood spooning coffee into a mug, and she deliberately kept her eyes on his hands instead of the wide expanse of bare chest which she could see beneath his unbuttoned shirt.

'I'd served my purpose, I think.'

Abbey studied him for a moment, taking in the lean hips and long, muscular legs and, when her eyes were irrevocably drawn to his, she said with quiet sincerity, 'I'm not like that, you know. I'm not in the habit of using people in the way you imagine.'

'I think you should leave, Miss Mitchell.' His voice was deep, and the words decisive. 'Your fiancé wouldn't like it if he found you here, and there are quite a few others, I imagine, who might have a great deal to say about it if they should know where you happen to be at this moment.'

'To the devil with Derek, and to the devil with the others!' she exclaimed, stamping her foot in a fit of rage she had last experienced as a child when she had found a stable boy lathering one of her favourite horses unnecessarily with a riding crop. 'If you want me to go, then say so, but don't use the others as an excuse!'

She was conscious of Hammond's narrowed eyes observing her dispassionately, but she was also conscious of the fact that she had meant every word she had said. They could *all* go to the devil; *including* Derek. During the past eighteen months Derek had decided where they would go, and when. When they had dined out, *he* had decided on the menu, and there had been occasions when he had actually told her what she should wear. She hadn't minded then, but she minded now when she realised with sudden clarity what marriage to Derek would mean. *He* would decide on whom she should be friends with, or whom she should associate with, and the frightening realisation, that she couldn't go through with it, hit her with a stunning force.

'Do you take milk and sugar in your coffee?' Hammond's voice interrupted her turbulent thoughts.

'Milk, but no sugar,' she replied automatically.

A mug was placed in her trembling hands and, for a brief moment, the rich aroma of coffee blended with the tantalising smell of his shaving cream, then he moved away from her and gestured abruptly towards the canvas chair a pace away from her.

'Sit down, you're shaking,' he ordered in a clipped voice and, to her horror, Abbey discovered that she was doing exactly that.

She was shaking so much that she was surprised her legs were still keeping her in an upright position and, lowering herself into the chair, she wrapped her hands around the mug in an effort to steady them.

'Does this mean you don't mind my being here?' she asked warily when she began to regain control of herself.

'I don't mind at all,' he smiled twistedly, and sipped at his steaming coffee as he sprawled in a chair close to hers. 'It isn't often I have a lovely young lady having early morning coffee with me.'

'You're not married, then?' she asked, vaguely judging his age somewhere between thirty and thirty-five as she tried to shake off her disturbing thoughts concerning Derek and herself.

'No,' Hammond shook his head and smiled faintly. 'Did you think I might have a wife tucked away somewhere there in the caravan?'

'I never really gave it a thought until now,' she admitted truthfully. 'Do you travel extensively?'

'Yes, I do.'

'I suppose you've been all over the country,' she probed casually, deciding that talking to him helped her not to think so much.

'Not all over, no,' he answered her query with equal casualness.

'Is this your first trip to Natal?'

'My second.' His glance settled on the engagement ring which sparkled on her finger, and something close to anger flashed in his grey-green eyes before he looked away and said abruptly, 'Drink your coffee.'

'Am I asking too many questions?'

She smiled at him tentatively, but there was no answering smile on his lips as he said: 'Your coffee is getting cold.'

Abbey drank her coffee in silence, and tried desperately not to think. She had been annoyed by a small avalanche of unpleasant incidents, but she would feel differently about the whole situation when she saw Derek again. The uncertainty and rebellion within her was merely a passing phase, and it *would* pass, she tried to tell herself.

'I'd better go,' she sighed eventually, reluctant to leave the tranquillity which seemed to surround his campsite, but the sun was climbing higher into the sky, and Nomad was becoming restless. Hammond accompanied her to where she had left her horse, and when she was safely in the saddle, her hands on the reins to keep Nomad in check, she looked down into Hammond's eyes and smiled a little selfconsciously. 'Thanks for the coffee, and it was nice meeting you, Hammond.'

He thrust the tips of his fingers into the pockets of his denims, and exposed a great deal more of his sun-browned chest in the process as he glanced up at her through eyes narrowed against the sun. 'Perhaps we'll meet again.'

'Perhaps,' she agreed vaguely, then she swung Nomad round and dug her heels into his flanks.

The horse responded at once, breaking into a canter until they reached the opposite side of the stream with its crystal clear water, then she gave Nomad the silent command he had waited for, and they sped across the earth to where the house was beginning to emerge among the tall trees.

Barney was there waiting for her when she reached the stable yard, and when she slid off Nomad's back he took the reins from her.

'Give him a good rub down, will you, Barney?' she said, caressing the horse's smooth neck.

'I'll do that, Miss Abbey,' Barney grinned at her toothily, but Abbey was already striding towards the house, her riding boots crunching on the gravel beneath her feet.

Edward Mitchell was in the kitchen, seated at the table with a cup of coffee in his hands, and his blue eyes smiled up at Abbey when she walked in.

'I was hoping you would have an opportunity to take Nomad out for a gallop,' he confided. 'He's been terribly irritable and restless lately, and he stubbornly refuses to tolerate anyone else on his back except you.'

'This morning's outing should last him for a while,' she replied, helping herself to a cup of coffee for fear that her father would think it strange if she didn't, then she joined him at the table. 'Is everyone else still asleep?'

'We got to bed late, remember,' Edward grinned. 'Not everyone enjoys rising as early as you and I do.'

'Dad ...' she began hesitantly, resting her elbows on the table, 'was it so terribly wrong of me to invite Hammond Scott to our engagement party last night?'

'You had a right to invite whom you pleased,' her father replied at once. 'His mode of dress might not have been suitable for the occasion, but his behaviour was impeccable.'

'There were some pretty nasty remarks floating about, and Dalene actually had the gall to attack him personally. I felt so ashamed and angry that I could willingly have slapped her.'

'Derek didn't like the idea that you'd invited Hammond, and neither did his parents.'

'Don't exclude Mother,' she reminded him bitterly.

'I wasn't going to, but you must try and understand how they felt, Abbey.' He smiled at the stubborn look that settled on her face. 'It was a meticulously planned, strictly formal affair and, even though I admire his courage, Hammond Scott was rather asking for unwanted attention when he walked in wearing denims.'

'I suppose so, yes,' she admitted reluctantly. 'He warned me that he didn't have an evening suit handy, but I told him that it didn't matter, and I think he finally accepted my invitation as some sort of a challenge.' She brushed her hair away from her face with an impatient hand as she added irritably, 'I still wish the Halsteads and Mother hadn't been so snooty about him being at the party.'

'Different people have a different set of standards by which they live, and who are we to criticise them?' her father remonstrated with her. 'They may not like our standards, but nothing in the world could make us change them, so they simply have to live with our peculiarities as we have to live with theirs.'

Abbey studied her father for a moment in thoughtful silence. 'What you're saying is that I must accept Derek and his people as they are, hoping that they will, in time, accept me as I am?'

'That's it,' her father nodded, but a frown slowly creased his brow. 'You haven't let this little incident upset you, have you?'

If only he knew how much, she thought, but instead she sighed and said: 'I guess I've seen a side of Derek during these last two days which I never realised existed before, and it will take a little time to get used to it.'

'You'll get used to it, my girl,' her father grinned, and somehow she knew that he was speaking from experience. 'You'll get used to it, you'll see.'

During the rest of that morning Abbey did very little except observe and listen as she deliberately focussed her attention on Derek and his family. It was as if she were seeing them all clearly for the first time, and what she saw she didn't like. They were stuffy and pompous, and so, she had to admit, was Derek.

Oh, why had she been so blind to it all in the past? she wondered frantically, but at the back of her mind there was a nagging little voice repeating the words, 'If you care enough for Derek, then none of this matters.'

When they returned to Durban after lunch that Sunday afternoon Derek did most of the talking while they travelled, and Abbey simply listened until she found herself nursing the most alarming thoughts.

They were nearing Durban when Derek said accusingly, 'You're much too impulsive, Abbey, and rather careless about whom you associate with, but we'll cure you of that.'

'We?' she asked stiffly, and with growing alarm.

'My parents and I,' he replied, unaware of the grimness of her expression.

'I see.'

'I mean, look at the way you invited that artist fellow to our engagement party,' Derek continued. 'As if that wasn't enough you still had to embarrass us all by making it quite clear to everyone that you approved of him attending the party dressed in that atrocious manner!'

Abbey turned her head away and stared unseeingly through the window at the scenery flashing past. 'Do you think we might change the subject?'

'Of course, darling.' His hand found hers in her lap and he squeezed it lightly. 'I didn't intend to sound reprimanding, but in future you must trust my judgement in these matters.'

This was exactly what she was afraid of. If she married Derek she would not only be losing her own identity, but she would be committing herself to a lifetime of having to trust his judgement in everything, even the type of friends she associated with, and there were only two things she could do about it. She could learn to live with it, as her father had suggested, or she could get out now while there was still time to do so.

'I must say I liked your mother's plans for the wedding, and my mother knows of a splendid place where you could do your shopping for a wedding gown,' Derek informed her enthusiastically. 'I've already told Mother what I considered would suit you.'

'Have you?' she asked uninterestedly, and not at all

surprised that he imagined he had a say in the kind of
wedding dress she should wear.

'We're going to have a wonderful wedding, Abbey. It
will be the kind of wedding people will talk about for
months and months afterwards.'

'Yes, I'm sure they will,' she murmured, but she had
almost convinced herself that people would be talking
about something totally different for some months to
come.

'You are excited about it, aren't you?' Derek asked
anxiously now, and she sighed heavily.

'At the moment I'm too tired to be excited about
anything,' she told him, and then neither of them spoke
during the last fifteen minutes of their journey.

When they finally stood facing each other in the
lounge of her flat, Derek drew her into his arms and
kissed her with his usual warmth, but, for the first time,
she felt nothing except irritation, and she wished he
would go and leave her in peace to sort out the tangled
web which had settled in her mind.

'Will I see you this evening?' he asked when at last he
released her.

'I don't think so. I have a lot to do.'

'I'll see you tomorrow evening, then,' he smiled,
dropping a light kiss on her forehead.

'That would be fine,' she agreed without enthusiasm,
and she sighed inwardly with relief when she found herself alone a few moments later.

What was she going to do? This question raged
through her mind for the rest of that afternoon, and a
large part of the evening. She eventually tried to weigh
Derek's good points up against his bad points, but that
only made matters worse, and when, at last, she went to
bed, she knew for certain that she had made a dreadful
mistake. She *couldn't* marry Derek. If she loved him

enough then these little quirks in his nature would have made no difference at all to her feelings for him, but she knew now that she had never loved him. She cared for him as a friend, yes, and she might have cared enough to consider marrying him, but, now that she saw him as he really was, she knew that marriage was something she could not enter into with him. She could not live with a man who would continually dictate to her whom she should mix with, or whom she should not speak to if they happened not to be in the same social class. It was disgusting, this prejudiced attitude in people who happened to be more fortunate than others.

'But what are you going to do?' the question surged to the forefront of her mind once more, and this time she knew that she had found the answer.

It was going to cause quite a disturbance, and she had no doubt that quite a few nasty remarks would be flung at her, but she would simply have to endure it. She would resign from her position in the architectural firm, and she would go home to Sweet Waters, but before she left she would give Derek's ring back to him. She would leave the latter for the last moment, mainly because she wanted to avoid his reproaches, but also because it would give her that much more time to make absolutely sure that, this time, she had made the right decision, and it was with this thought that her mind came to rest, allowing her to go to sleep.

Abbey handed in her resignation first thing on the Monday morning, and with a little effort she managed to persuade her dismayed employer that he should let her go within two weeks instead of a month. Her resignation caused a stir among the staff, but that did not trouble her as much as attempting to appear natural in Derek's company and, consequently, she tried to avoid seeing him as much as possible. She had made no plans as yet for the future, but she would have plenty of time during her stay at Sweet Waters to decide what she was going to do.

Derek telephoned her one afternoon during her last week at the office. He invited her to dine at his parents' home that evening, but she declined with the excuse that she would be dining with a few of her friends at the office. This was, of course, not the truth, but in view of what she was contemplating it would not seem right to have dinner with his parents, and neither had she any desire to see them again. She could not, however, escape having lunch with Derek the following day, but she was not looking forward to it at all.

They had lunch at Maxim's, their usual meeting place, and when at last the reached the coffee stage, Derek said unsuspectingly, 'Mother and I have been discussing the wedding, and we've both decided that Dalene would look good as a bridesmaid in pale blue.'

This was the last straw, Abbey told herself. If she had harboured any doubts about breaking off her engagement to Derek, then she no longer had them. Dalene as her bridesmaid? *Over her dead body!*

'I was going to ask my friend Rosemary Hill to be bridesmaid,' she replied, simply for the sake of arguing.

'That's out of the question,' Derek brushed aside the idea at once with a stubborn look on his handsome face. 'It's all been arranged. Dalene will act as bridesmaid, and my cousin Walter will be best man.'

There was no point in arguing further; she had made her decision, after all, and in a few days' time none of this would matter.

Derek tried to kiss her when they parted company a few minutes later, but Abbey turned her head swiftly, and his kiss landed somewhere on her cheek. His eyebrows rose enquiringly, but if they did not hurry they would both be late at their respective offices, and Abbey was spared having to think up an acceptable explanation.

On the Friday, her last day at the office, she telephoned Derek and asked him to meet her for lunch.

'I'll see you at the usual place,' he said agreeably, but this time Abbey was in a rebellious mood.

'Not the usual place,' she said quickly. 'I'll meet you at the Pirates' Den. It's quiet there, and we can talk.'

She returned the receiver to its cradle before he could protest, but there was a hollow, slightly nervous feeling at the pit of her stomach, and it persisted throughout the rest of the morning.

The Pirates' Den was quiet, as Abbey had said, but she nevertheless chose a corner table where they could also be reasonably private. The food was excellent, Derek could not fault that, but she could see that he disapproved the fact that the restaurant had been one of her choice, and it merely made her all the more determined to end this brief engagement of theirs.

'You chose this place so that we could talk, but for the past half hour I seem to have done most of the talking while you've hardly anything to say,' Derek reminded her at length.

He smiled, and it was a handsome, boyish smile which made it all the more difficult for her to do what she knew she had to do, but she realised that she had stalled long enough.

'If I could make it any easier for you, Derek, then believe me I would, but there's no sense in beating about the bush,' she said, pushing her plate aside and meeting his glance squarely. 'I want to break off our engagement.'

'You want to *what*?' Derek demanded, his face paling visibly as he stared at her incredulously, and at that moment she pitied him in a way she had never done before.

'I can't marry you, Derek,' she replied quietly, but firmly.

'But—but why not?' he blustered. 'What's made you change your mind?'

'Several things.'

His brown eyes darkened with anger, and something she did not like. 'One of them, I suppose, is that artist fellow.'

'Hammond Scott has nothing to do with this at all,' she denied sharply.

'Then why?'

'I couldn't live with a man who would rule my life as completely as you would rule mine, Derek.' There was a hint of anger in her voice at that moment to match the anger in his eyes. 'You would deny me the choice of my own friends, just as you've very cleverly denied me the choice of a wedding dress and bridesmaid, for a start, and that's what I can't tolerate.'

'Listen to me, Abbey.' He leaned forward across the table, his hand reaching out for hers, but she evaded his touch. 'I shan't interfere in your choice of friends, and I'll leave the choice of wedding dress and bridesmaid to you, but please, darling, don't throw away our happiness in this careless way.'

Her mouth was set in a determined line as she shook her head. 'It won't work, Derek.'

'How can you say that?' he demanded anxiously.

'I can say it because it's true,' she insisted adamantly. 'You didn't like the idea that I was friendly with a man like Hammond Scott because your considered him beneath our status, but that wasn't enough. You were extremely rude to him for no reason at all, and I think that was when I began to see you as you really are. It made me take a closer look at you, and it made me think.'

'Abbey . . .'

'I'm sorry, Derek.' She pulled the ostentatious diamond ring off her finger, and passed it to him across the table. 'It was a mistake from the start, and I blame myself entirely for not realising it sooner.'

'Perhaps you need time to reconsider,' he suggested hopefully, his hands shaking as he picked up the ring and twisted it between his fingers.

'I've given it more than enough thought, and you might as well know that I've also resigned my job. I'm leaving Durban tomorrow morning to spend a few weeks with my family.'

Derek slipped the ring into his pocket and frowned angrily. 'Hammond Scott will be there as well.'

'So he will,' she retorted, sensing the trend of his thoughts, 'but I doubt if I shall see him and, quite frankly, I couldn't care less whether I do or not.'

'I thought you loved me, Abbey,' he said, a hurt look flashing across his white, sensitive face.

'I was mistaken.' She lowered her eyes, no longer able to face him, and, picking up her handbag, she rose to her feet. 'Goodbye, Derek.'

'Wait a minute!' His hand captured hers as she passed his chair, and when she glanced down at him she had the most awful suspicion that he was going to cry, but he obviously pulled himself together. 'It can't just end like this!' he protested urgently.

'There's no sense in prolonging the inevitable,' she told him gently as she disengaged her hand from his. 'I'm sorry.'

Derek did not follow her as she walked out of the restaurant, and she felt considerably lighter when she stepped out into the busy street. She was free, and although she regretted having had to hurt Derek in the process, she was certain now that she had made the right decision. All that remained was for her to tell her parents that there would be no wedding, and that was something she did not look forward to. She could only hope that they would understand, and forgive her.

Abbey began her journey at dawn the Saturday morning, and her little red Porsche picked up speed as soon as she left the city behind her. She was going home, but she had not quite decided how long she would stay in those familiar and picturesque surroundings. All she wanted at that moment was to put as much distance as possible between Derek and herself, and the chained existence she would have led as his wife. She had been a fool not to realise it before, but Derek had very subtly dominated her life from the very beginning of their relationship, and because of this she had lost contact with many dear and wonderful friends – his autocratic manner had made certain of that.

She had been blinded by his tenderness and his obvious concern fo ne well-being, but his true nature he had kept well hidden until that weekend at Sweet Waters when they had become engaged. Fortunately she had realised her mistake in time, and she knew now why she had never been able to tell him that she loved him. If she had to be truthful with herself, then she was forced to admit that she never had and never could love him.

Love! There it was again, that much used word which conjured up such mysterious emotions. Would she ever know its true meaning, or would she always be left to wonder?

A shuddering sigh escaped her, and she concentrated on her driving, trying to rid herself of these troublesome thoughts, but she could not prevent herself from thinking of how she had travelled this way two weeks ago with such happy notions of marrying Derek. That vision of peace and contentment had been swiftly and rudely shattered, and she could not understand why she had not seen through Derek much sooner. Why, oh, why did it have to happen only *after* their engagement? There had been that elaborate party with all those influential people to witness the occasion, and she could just imagine how the tongues would wag once the news leaked out that there was going to be no wedding after all.

'Oh, damn them all!' she muttered loudly to herself. She could only hope that her parents would understand, and that she could rely on their support, for she most certainly would need it.

When Eagle's Peak came into view later that morning, Abbey found it a welcoming sight, and it eased some of the tension which had knotted her insides during these past two weeks. Soon, very soon, she would be at Sweet Waters, and then she could relax completely. In these peaceful surroundings she could shake off the memory of her mistaken dreams of happiness, and here she would find the necessary courage to face the future once more.

Her father was emerging from the house at the precise moment when her Porsche roared up the drive, and he stopped in his stride until she had parked her car. Moments later Abbey hurled herself into her father's arms, and buried her face against his solid, comforting shoulder.

'We didn't expect you, my girl,' he said with a smile in his voice as he kissed her cheek and hugged her close, 'but it's good to have you here for the weekend.'

At the mention of the word 'weekend' Abbey disengaged herself from his arms and looked away selfconsciously. 'Is Mother in the house?'

'I left her in the kitchen supervising lunch.' Edward

placed a heavy arm about her shoulders and smiled wickedly. 'Shall we go in and surprise her?'

'Yes,' Abbey nodded warily, wondering agitatedly what he would say when he was faced with the surprise *she* had in store for them. 'I have something to tell you both.'

CHAPTER FOUR

CLAIRE MITCHELL had served tea in her delicate china cups, and the conversation was somehow stilted until Abbey placed her empty cup on the small table beside her chair. It was then that Edward and Claire noticed the absence of Abbey's engagement ring, and an abrupt silence settled in the living-room which was disturbed only, it seemed, by the nervous beating of Abbey's heart when she realised that her announcement could no longer be delayed.

'There's going to be no wedding,' she said, her voice echoing through the silent room as she observed the expressions on her parents' faces.

Her father's leathery features registered shock, but he remained surprisingly calm. Her mother's face, however, looked white and stricken, and her grey eyes sliced through Abbey as she demanded, 'What do you mean, there's going to be no wedding?'

'I've broken off my engagement to Derek.'

'Have you gone quite mad, Abbey?' Claire shrieked at her. 'How could you do such a thing after all the expense and the trouble we took with your engagement party?'

'Just a minute, Claire,' Edward intervened calmly.

'I'm sure Abbey has an explanation to back up her decision.'

'There's no explanation which could suffice for her outrageous behaviour!' Claire snorted furiously, and Abbey felt her mouth go dry.

'There's nothing outrageous, Mother, about realising in time that one has made a mistake.'

'For goodness' sake, Abbey!' Her mother rose to her feet and paced the floor irritably while Abbey and her father remained seated. 'Most girls would have given everything they possessed for a man like Derek. He's from a wealthy, influential family, and in not so many years from now he'll be at the head of his father's firm. Besides, I've always considered him extremely presentable in every other way.'

There was a hint of defiance in Abbey's raised glance. 'I'm sorry, Mother, but I'm not going to let any man take control of my life as completely as Derek would have done.'

'Take over your life?' Claire shouted incredulously. 'What on earth are you talking about?'

'Dominate is perhaps a better word,' Abbey supplemented.

'Dominate?' Her mother paused in front of her. 'Don't be ridiculous! He's never dominated you in any way.'

'Oh, yes, he has, but it was all done very subtly at first. That weekend we became engaged was an eye-opener to me in many ways,' Abbey argued, her anger rising sharply. 'I would be denied the freedom of my own judgement, just as I've been denied the choice of my own wedding dress and bridesmaid. Derek and his mother have gone ahead with the arrangements, and it's all been done without their stopping to consult me.'

'But what's wrong with that?' her mother demanded

impatiently. 'Jeanette Halstead has impeccable taste, and Dalene would be absolutely perfect as your bridesmaid.'

Abbey glanced up at her mother with a measure of distaste. 'So you know about Dalene being their choice?'

'We discussed it the weekend of your engagement, and I had no objections. Dalene is a delightful girl.'

Abbey leapt to her feet, almost forgetting the presence of her father as she faced Claire furiously. 'Dalene is a bitch!'

'Abigail! Your language!' her mother gasped in horror.

'To hell with my language!' Abbey spat out the words, clenching her shaking hands at her sides. 'Dalene is a vindictive bitch who not only insulted the one person I invited to our engagement party, but she made it her business to give the impression that I'd deliberately invited Hammond Scott to disrupt the arrangements for the evening—and, what's more, Derek stood by and allowed her to continue without making the slightest effort to stop her.'

Claire gestured disparagingly. 'You had no right to invite Mr Scott here that evening.'

'I had *every* right!' Abbey insisted heatedly, ignoring her father's gestures that she should calm down. 'You invited your friends, and so did the Halsteads. It was only when I started thinking things over that I discovered how cleverly I'd been prevented from drawing up a list of the friends I would have wanted to invite, but, like Hammond Scott, they wouldn't have been classy enough or rich enough for you and the Halsteads, and that's what has disgusted me so much.'

'Well, really! I don't——'

'Just a minute, Claire,' her father intervened calmly.

'I think we've stepped off the subject slightly.' His blue glance rested on Abbey once more. 'Why, precisely, have you broken off your engagement?'

Abbey sighed tiredly, and sat down on the arm of the chair she had vacated. 'From the moment we became engaged I realised that it was all wrong, and when we left here that Sunday I already knew that I couldn't go through with it. Derek's behaviour that weekend made me realise that I hadn't really known him at all, and when I took a closer look at him I found that I didn't like what I saw.' She lowered her eyes to her hands which were clenched so tightly in her lap. 'These other little things, such as denying me the choice of what I should wear, and so on, merely helped to convince me that marrying him would be a mistake.' She sighed again, and spread her hands out in an appealing, yet helpless gesture. 'I feel terrible about it, but there it is.'

'I shudder to think what the Halsteads must think of us,' Claire remarked coldly.

'The Halsteads may think what they please,' Edward stated with an unfamiliar harshness in his voice as he, too, rose to his feet. 'It's our daughter's happiness that counts.'

There was an ominous silence as her parents' glances clashed, and Abbey swallowed nervously. 'There's something else I have to tell you,' she said, capturing their attention once more. 'I've resigned my job, and I'm staying home for a while until this has all blown over.'

Her mother's mouth twisted cynically. 'You've come home to hide, you mean.'

'Claire,' Edward exclaimed, his voice a harsh reprimand when he saw Abbey flinch, but nothing would stop her mother once she was in this condescending, spiteful mood.

'I came home because I'd hoped you would understand, but it seems as though I was mistaken,' Abbey explained stiffly.

'Well, if you expected me to pat you on the shoulder and tell you what a good girl you are, then you were definitely mistaken,' her mother snapped. 'Personally, I think you've gone quite out of your mind.'

'That will do, Claire!' Edward thundered furiously. 'I suggest you make us a fresh pot of tea.'

Abbey had never heard her father speak this harshly to her mother before, and she thought for a moment that her mother was going to ignore his command, but she snatched up the teapot and marched out of the living-room, leaving Abbey alone with her father.

'Come here, my girl,' Edward said gently, taking in the tears which hovered on Abbey's lashes and, when she had walked into his comforting arms, he said with astonishing shrewdness, 'The truth is, you never really loved Derek.'

'I thought I did, but I've come to the conclusion that I don't really know what love is,' she cried, burying her face against him. 'Oh, Dad, I've made such a mess of things!'

'There now,' he patted her soothingly. 'Don't upset yourself.'

'I felt so terrible having to hurt Derek,' she confessed when at last she had regained a measure of her control.

'I know,' Edward nodded, drawing her towards the sofa and sitting down beside her. 'But just think how much he would have been hurt if you'd waited until after your marriage, and you know how messy a divorce would have been.'

Abbey shook her head and dried her eyes with the handkerchief her father had pushed into her hands. 'I couldn't let it go that far.'

'And you were right,' he agreed, smiling at her. 'Dry your tears. I can hear your mother coming, and don't pay too much attention to her. She'll get over it in time.'

'Here's the tea,' Claire announced moments later, placing the tea pot on the trolley, and her face mirrored her displeasure. 'I suggest you pour, Abbey. I have things to see to in the kitchen.'

She left them as abruptly as she had arrived, and Abbey and her father stared at each other for a while in resigned silence.

'I've really done it this time, haven't I?' she smiled shakily as she poured the tea and handed her father his cup.

'Didn't I teach you to always stick to your decisions and, if you found that you'd made a mistake, to have the courage to admit it?'

'Yes,' she nodded.

'Well then?'

'Thanks, Dad.' Her smile broadened at last, dispersing the shadows in her eyes. 'I feel a whole lot better now.'

Abbey could recall happier times she had spent at Sweet Waters, and this weekend had certainly not been one of them. The atmosphere had been strained as a result of her mother's attitude, and no matter how much Abbey and her father had tried to remonstrate with her, Claire remained of the opinion that Abbey did not know what she was doing.

With her father out of the house on the Monday morning, Abbey could not take the long, drawn-out silences between her mother and herself, and she eventually went for a long walk. She did not particularly care which direction she took, but some time later she found herself at the waterfall with its clear pool, smooth rocks, and shady trees. She had come there often as a child to watch the water emerging from a gaping hole in the rocks to fall fifty feet down into a natural pool which overflowed, in turn, into the stream which sliced Sweet Waters in two.

She seated herself on a large, flat rock and, with the sound of the gushing water in her ears, she stared out across the pool, idly watching the sun shimmering on the crystal-clear water where a dragonfly skimmed low several times before darting off elsewhere. She had sat there once with Derek, allowing him to persuade her that she should marry him, but she did not want to think of Derek, and the terrible mistake she had made in agreeing to become his wife. That was behind her now, and she wanted to forget it, but his hurt expression would linger in her memory for a long time yet. She had never in her life hurt anyone deliberately, but hurting Derek had been unavoidable under the circumstances.

She stared moodily into the distance, seeing nothing until a flat pebble skipped across the water, and she glanced quickly over her shoulder to see Hammond Scott standing some distance from her with his thumbs hooked into the wide belt which hugged his khaki pants to his lean hips. The bulging muscles in his wide shoulders and chest were clearly visible beneath the faded green sweater, and his coppery hair lay in its usual untidy fashion across his broad forehead.

'I've been watching you for quite some time,' his deep, pleasant voice remarked, and his grey-green eyes mocked her slightly. 'You're not thinking of drowning yourself, are you?'

'That would be rather difficult,' she replied stiffly, not quite sure how she felt about this intrusion into her privacy. 'I'm an excellent swimmer.'

'I'm very glad to hear that.' His mouth twitched slightly and, without asking her permission, he seated himself on the rock beside her. 'Are you on holiday?'

'I've resigned my job,' she stated bluntly, not quite knowing why she should enlighten him to this extent, and moving a little away from him when his shoulder brushed against her own.

'I get it,' Hammond smiled, his glance faintly cynical as it rested on her. 'You've decided to sit out the length of your engagement here at your home, and you're already missing your fiancé.'

'I no longer have a fiancé.'

Before she could prevent him he took possession of her left hand to observe for himself the absence of her magnificent ring, and once again the cynical expression flitted across his rugged face.

'It didn't take him long to feel the pinch of the noose around his neck, I must say, but it was clever of him to make his escape while he still had the time,' he observed drily, and Abbey wrenched her hand from his angrily.

'He didn't end the engagement,' she explained bitterly. 'I did.'

'Well, they say it's a woman's prerogative to change her mind, and women tend to make full use of it.'

'No need to ask whose side you're on,' she replied accusingly to his mocking statement. 'When a man changes his mind he's being wise, but when a woman does so she's merely acting on a foolish whim.'

'I never said that.'

'But you implied it,' she insisted, her blue eyes sparkling with suppressed anger.

'Stop being so touchy,' he laughed harshly. 'Instead of sitting here moping, let's celebrate your freedom.'

One hand raised her chin while the other cupped the back of her head, and before she had time to realise what he was up to, he was kissing her firmly on the mouth.

'Why did you do that?' she asked dazedly, her lips still tingling with the remembered pressure of his mouth.

'I've wanted to kiss you since the first moment I saw you, and this seemed to be the appropriate time,' he shrugged, a gleam of mockery leaping in his peculiar eyes. 'Did you like it?'

She coloured swiftly and looked away. 'I—I don't know.'

'Shall I kiss you again to help you decide?'

'I don't think so,' she said quickly, raising her hands in a defensive action when he leaned towards her purposefully. 'Thanks all the same.'

His eyes lingered on her lips, and she experienced the strangest fluttering in her breast. For one ridiculous moment she actually wanted him to kiss her again, then she pulled herself together sharply, and averted her glance once more.

'Will you let me paint a portrait of you?'

'What?' Abbey asked, staring at him now with an incredulous look on her face.

'Such beautiful ears couldn't possibly be deaf,' he observed smoothly, brushing her hair away from her face with a lazy finger to expose one small, shell-like ear. 'Will you let me paint a portrait of you?' he repeated his question tolerantly.

'I think you're crazy,' she laughed nervously, evading his touch.

'I'd be crazy not to,' he contradicted, his eyes travelling over her with slow, systematic interest. 'Beautiful hair, good bone structure, enchanting eyes, very kissable lips, and——'

'That's enough!' she stopped him abruptly when his

glance dipped down towards the curve of her breasts beneath her thin cotton blouse, and the amused twitch of his lips did not escape her attention.

'Will you sit for me?' he persisted.

'I think I need time to get used to the idea first,' she evaded the subject, and he laughed incredulously.

'Most women would be vain enough to leap at the opportunity of having their features immortalised on canvas.'

'Really?'

Her sarcasm lit the light of mockery in his eyes. 'You don't fancy being immortalised?'

'I've never considered myself subject matter for a portrait,' she replied with sudden honesty.

'You don't see yourself as I see you.'

'And how do you see me?' she questioned his tantalising remark.

'Let me do your portrait, then you'll be able to see for yourself,' he said persuasively, tempting her to accept.

'I have a niggling suspicion that I'm being lured into a trap.'

'The only thing I want to trap is your image on canvas,' Hammond assured her, and this time his glance was challenging. 'Are you going to deny me the privilege?'

She stared at him for a long time, trying to decide what to do, then she shrugged carelessly, and sighed; 'What have I got to lose?'

'We'll start tomorrow,' said Hammond as he rose to his feet, then he pointed down at the ground and added abruptly, 'Here, at eight-thirty, and don't be late.'

Abbey watched him disappear amongst the trees with a bemused smile on her lips, and then she was alone once more with the sound of rushing water in her ears.

Hammond Scott was absolutely one of the strangest men she had ever met, and she could not decide whether she ought to like him or hate him.

She sat there for a long time, remembering his kiss, and she felt again that odd fluttering in her breast. His mouth had been warm and firm when it had taken command of hers for those brief seconds, and if she had to be honest with herself, then she would admit that she had actually enjoyed his kiss.

The sun was high in the sky when Abbey arrived back at the house, and her mother's sharp glance did not miss the dry grass clinging to her skirt.

'Where were you this morning?' Claire demanded sharply, her suspicious glance raking Abbey from head to foot.

'I took a walk out to the waterfall,' Abbey told her, brushing the evidence of her stroll from her skirt before she entered the house and poured herself an iced lime drink.

Claire followed her into the living-room, and the air was all at once crackling with tension when she faced Abbey and said: 'I suppose you knew that Mr Scott would be sketching in that area.'

'I didn't know,' Abbey admitted truthfully, drinking her iced lime thirstily, and discovering at last the reason for her mother's agitation.

'You saw him, I presume?'

'Yes,' Abbey nodded, 'and we talked for a while.'

'What about?'

'Really, Mother!' Abbey snapped angrily, returning her empty glass with unnecessary force to the tray. 'Since when do I have to give you a detailed account of my conversation with people?'

Claire's mouth tightened ominously. 'I'm merely concerned about you, Abbey, and I wouldn't want you to become involved with the wrong kind of people.'

'Involved?' Abbey demanded indignantly. 'What kind of involvement do you envisage, and what, may I know, is wrong with Hammond Scott?'

'Well, he's—he's only staying here at Sweet Waters for a very short while.'

'Be a little more explicit, Mother,' Abbey insisted, her anger being fanned into a raging fury.

'Do I have to spell it out for you?' Claire demanded.

'I wish you would!'

'The man's a total stranger to us,' her mother began. 'We don't know whether he has any family worth mentioning, or whether, in fact, he simply sprang up in a gutter somewhere.'

'I'm surprised you haven't made it your business to find out these things,' Abbey hissed, almost choking on the words in her fury.

'One simply has to look at him to see what he is,' Claire continued coldly. 'He's a drifter, and like all drifters he'll never have a cent to his name, nor a reasonable position in society.'

'Wealth and status!' Abbey spat out the words as if they were vile objects in her mouth. 'That's all you really care about, isn't it! Because Hammond Scott so obviously doesn't bear the stamp of your elevated society he's condemned on the spot!'

'No self-respecting person would live the way he's living,' Claire argued stubbornly.

'He has a home in Johannesburg, you know,' Abbey defended Hammond sarcastically.

'Has he?' her mother demanded with equal sarcasm. 'I can imagine what it must look like.'

Abbey took a deep, steadying breath, then she said coldly, 'It hasn't occurred to you, I suppose, that there are many decent, law-abiding citizens among the not so wealthy?'

Claire snorted disparagingly. 'I've never had the desire to crawl into their hovels in order to find out.'

'It's pointless arguing with you,' Abbey snapped, seething with inward rage as she brushed past her mother.

'Abbey!' That cold, high-pitched voice halted her long before the could reach the door. 'You will stay out of Mr Scott's way.'

Abbey turned slowly to face her mother, and her expression was as determined as Claire's. 'I have no intention of carrying out your high-handed instruction, Mother. As a matter of fact, I shall be seeing quite a lot of him from now on. He's asked to do a portrait of me, and I've agreed.'

'What's this about a portrait?' Edward demanded, entering the living-room so silently that neither Abbey nor her mother had heard him.

'Hammond Scott wants to do a portrait of me,' Abbey repeated her statement in a considerably calmer voice.

'Why, that's wonderful,' Edward smiled, placing an arm about Abbey's shoulders and hugging her briefly.

'How can you encourage her in this respect, Edward?' Claire demanded in an outraged voice.

'My dear Claire,' her husband sighed, 'the man wants to do her portrait, nothing more, and if Abbey is agreeable to it, then why not let him?'

Claire's mouth tightened into a thin line of angry disapproval. 'I've forbidden her to associate with the man.'

'For goodness' sake! There's nothing wrong with Hammond Scott!' Edward remarked in a voice harsh with anger, but Claire was equally angry.

'What do you know about him?' she demanded shrilly.

'I've taken the trouble to get to know him in the way

I take the trouble to get to know the people who work for me, and I like what I've seen of this man.' Edward paused abruptly, his brows drawing together in a frown as he faced his wife. 'Hammond Scott is not the brainless nincompoop you take him for, and I see no reason why our daughter shouldn't associate with him if she wants to.'

'But——'

'The subject is closed,' Edward interrupted Claire in an authoritative voice, then he turned towards the door and said irritably, 'Let's eat. It's late, and I still have to check on the tanks this afternoon before we can start dipping the cattle tomorrow.'

The tension in the house climbed higher, and after lunch Abbey accompanied her father to where the cattle would be dipped the following morning. Anything was better than staying in the house with her mother, and although she was not of much help to her father, she remained there with him, enjoying the peace and the quiet of the afternoon as she watched him carry out his inspection.

'I can't understand your mother's attitude,' he said at length, taking out his pipe and lighting it. 'But then, I suppose, I've never really understood her.'

Abbey listened, but kept her opinions to herself. She loved her mother, but she could not tolerate her prejudiced attitude, and this was the reason they clashed so often. If only she would unbend a little, Abbey thought ruefully, but she supposed that would be asking for too much.

'She's up to something,' her father interrupted her thoughts, and Abbey looked up to see him puffing furiously at his pipe. 'I can sense it in the air. She's up to something, and I don't think I'm going to like it.'

He was, of course, referring to her mother, and that

gnawing sensation intensified at the pit of her stomach. Her father was never wrong where it concerned her mother, and knowing this filled Abbey with nervous apprehension for the future.

Abbey left the house early the following morning to keep her appointment with Hammond, but when she arrived at the waterfall she found that he had already set up his easel and was leaning against a tree, smoking a cigarette while he waited for her.

'Am I late?' she asked, conscious of her heartbeat quickening ridiculously at the sight of him.

'You're two minutes early, actually,' he announced after consulting his watch, then his critical glance slid down the length of her.

'You never said what you wanted me to wear,' she said, gesturing selfconsciously to her slacks and blouse.

'Wear whatever you like, and not necessarily the same thing every time,' he replied absently, then he gestured her towards the rock. 'Will you sit where you were sitting yesterday?'

She obeyed in silence, grateful for the shade of the trees at that time of the morning on that particular rock.

'Turn your head slightly towards your left,' Hammond instructed.

'Like this?' she asked nervously, staring out across the pool.

'That's it,' he said abruptly, his canvas shoes making no sound on the grass as he walked towards her, then he seated himself beside her and raised a hand to the scarf which she had used to tie her hair back. His eyes met hers enquiringly. 'Do you mind?'

'No,' she whispered, conscious of the clean male smell of him as he untied the scarf and arranged her hair so that it trailed thickly across one shoulder.

'You have lovely hair.'

'So you said yesterday,' she replied flippantly.

'And I shall say it again tomorrow,' he smiled mockingly, and she stiffened at the tremor that raced along her nerves when his hand brushed against her throat. She was not sure whether his touch had been deliberate, but he withdrew his hand at once and walked towards his easel. From a shabby suitcase he selected the items he would require, and it was only when he straightened that he glanced critically in her direction again. 'Relax, Abbey, and let your thoughts go. I want to see them flitting across your face in the same way they did yesterday.'

His voice was low, and oddly persuasive, and she found herself obeying. A bee buzzed around her, but she remained perfectly still while Hammond worked. How good was he at doing portraits? she wondered casually, recalling her own meagre efforts to capture the image of a few of her friends on paper. Some of her efforts had been hilarious, but others had been remarkably accurate, even if she had to say so herself.

'Am I allowed to talk?' she asked at length when the rush of water cascading into the pool lulled her to the verge of drowsiness.

'Be my guest,' Hammond replied, glancing up at her from time to time as he worked, but when she could think of nothing to say he started the conversation with the most unexpected query. 'What made you change your mind about marrying your fancy boy-friend?'

'That's a personal matter,' she replied, stiffening with distaste.

'Did he try to make love to you?'

'Certainly not!'

'Perhaps that was his mistake.'

The mockery in his voice made her say testily, 'Sex had nothing to do with my reason for breaking off our engagement.'

'There's nothing wrong with sex, you know,' he assured her in that same mocking tone. 'It's a very natural and beautiful thing between a man and a woman.'

'So I'm told,' she retorted stiffly, her cheeks growing warmer.

Sex was not a subject she had ever been able to discuss freely with anyone, and she had certainly never discussed it with Derek; not even during their most intimate moments. She laughed inwardly now at her use of the word 'intimate'. The moments of intimacy shared with Derek had consisted of light kisses and casual caresses. He had been too much of a gentleman to ever think of touching her intimately, and that was perhaps the reason why she had felt so safe and comfortable with him; why she had, in fact, allowed herself to consider marrying him. Hammond was right in a way, she thought distractedly. Had Derek perhaps tried to make love to her, then she might have discovered sooner that she did not care for him in that way at all.

'This is the most unusual waterfall I've ever seen,' Hammond's deep voice interrupted her thoughts.

'The water falls into a crevice somewhere high up in the mountain, and the crevice eventually becomes a tunnel which leads towards this outlet,' she explained, grateful to him for directing her thoughts along a different channel. 'Legend has it that a dragon lived in that cave-like opening, and it's believed that once a month he used to come down out of his cave to capture a maiden bathing in this natural pool. The Zulus call the waterfall "maiden's tears". The maidens have never stopped weeping, you see, since the dragon took them into captivity.'

'The Zulu tribes in this area surely don't still cling to that old belief?' Hammond laughed mockingly, and she shook her head.

'Not the younger ones who are more educated, but they speak of it in the same manner we might speak of fairy tales.' She rose without thinking and kneeled at the water's edge, scooping out water in her cupped hands, and letting it trickle through her fingers. 'The water is clear, and has been purified in nature's own unique way. It's sweet, too, and naturally that's why my grandfather named this farm "Sweet Waters".'

'Abbey,' Hammond sighed exasperatedly, 'get back to that rock, and sit still so that I can get on with the preliminaries of this portrait.'

'Sorry,' she muttered apologetically, doing as she was told, and they were silent for a long time after that.

Abbey watched the dragonflies darting across the water, but her thoughts were at home with her mother, who was so against her sitting for this portrait. 'She's up to something,' she recalled her father's words, and that hateful tension once again knotted her insides.

'Relax,' Hammond ordered, sensing the change in her mood, but when, a few minutes later, she was still rigid with tension, he crossed the space between them in a few long strides, and sat down beside her. 'What's wrong?' he demanded tersely.

'Nothing,' she snapped, but when she looked up into his compelling eyes she heard herself say agitatedly, 'Oh, everything's wrong, and I regret coming home.'

'Tell me about it,' Hammond instructed quietly. 'Why did you come home?'

'I came,' she explained, 'because I'd hoped my parents would understand, but I'm afraid only my father has shown me the understanding I needed so desperately.

My mother . . .' She swallowed convulsively and tried again. 'My mother has done nothing except rant and rave about the unnecessary expense and the shame of a broken engagement. She thinks I've gone mad, and that's all there is to it.' She drew a steadying breath and looked away from him. 'I don't know why I'm telling you all this, but my father said something yesterday that bothers me. He said that my mother was up to something, and I wish to heaven I knew what it was.'

'Perhaps she's going to attempt a reconciliation between you and your fiancé.'

'There will be no reconciliation,' she exclaimed stubbornly, a tremor of anxiety racing through her as she considered Hammond's suggestion.

'Are you absolutely sure that you've made the right decision this time?'

'Absolutely!'

She raised her eyes in a silent appeal that he should believe her, and the next moment his lips swooped down on to hers in a kiss that seemed to set every nerve in her body tingling. She tried to draw away, but his arms went about her in that instant as if he had anticipated her move, and she was crushed against his hard chest while his mouth explored hers with an intimacy which both alarmed and excited her. There was no hesitancy in his manner; no fumbling uncertainty in the lips that ravaged hers, nor the hands that held and caressed her so effortlessly. This man was no inexperienced youth, she realised with some dismay, and he was drawing a response from her which she could not suppress even if she had wanted to. She had been kissed before, but never had the touch of a man's lips awakened such wild emotions within her, and her heart was beating so fast that she could hardly breath when he finally released her.

'Let's get back to work,' he ordered abruptly as if nothing unusual had happened, and she felt curiously deflated at the discovery that he could appear so unaffected by what had occurred.

CHAPTER FIVE

HAMMOND worked on in silence. When the preliminary sketch was completed, he started on the oils, the stroke of his brushes swift, accurate, and confident. He knew what he was doing, Abbey was aware of that, and her curiosity about him could no longer be contained.

'Tell me about yourself?' she broke the lengthy silence between them when she had summoned up sufficient courage, and his eyebrows rose cynically.

'Are you asking for the history of my life?'

'You may skip the details and tell me whatever you want me to know,' she shrugged, attempting to look casual.

'I'm thirty-three, I have a sister some years older than myself who's married with a family of her own, and my parents died when both my sister and I were small children,' he rattled off the information as if it were a well-rehearsed rhyme he kept in reserve for those who dared to probe into his private life. 'We were looked after by an uncle until we were old enough to stand on our own two feet,' he added as an afterthought.

'Is your uncle still alive?'

'He died five years ago.'

'I'm sorry.'

'Don't be,' he said abruptly, stepping back to view his work critically. 'My uncle was old, and he'd lived a very full and interesting life. He was ready to go, and in the end, I think, he was impatient for it.'

He had spoken the words in an extraordinary callous way, and she decided to change the subject. 'If you make a living out of painting, why have I never seen any of your work exhibited before?'

'I've never exhibited any of my work,' he stated bluntly.

'But then——'

'I sell a painting here and there, and it keeps me going,' he interrupted, guessing her query, then he surprised her further by saying, 'I'm actually in the throes of planning my first exhibition.

'Are you?' she asked, turning to face him as her interest quickened.

'Sit still, and for goodness' sake don't fidget!'

'Sorry,' she gulped, resuming her original position. 'When are you planning to have this exhibition?'

'In two, perhaps three months' time.' He frowned down at the canvas. 'It depends on how soon I'm ready for it.'

'I suppose it will be held in Johannesburg,' she sighed, arching her back carefully.

'That's right.' He looked up then, and smiled faintly. 'Are you tired?'

'A little,' she confessed with a grimace.

'I think we'd better stop for the day,' he announced, packing away his brushes and paints. 'The sun is shifting, and the light is not as I would wish it.'

Abbey rose to her feet and arched her back once more in an effort to ease the aching stiffness, then she strolled towards the easel. 'May I see what you've done?'

'No!' he said harshly, swinging round to face her, and his forbidding expression made her halt abruptly.

'Why not?' she asked, caught between surprise and

disappointment. 'Aren't you going to let me see it at all?'

'You may see it when it's finished.'

She tilted her head up at him to observe him in thoughtful silence for a moment, then she asked gravely, 'Is that a promise?'

'I promise that no one shall have the privilege of seeing this portrait unless you've seen it first,' he said, raising his right hand as if he were taking an oath, and smiling down at her mockingly. 'How's that?'

'That's all right with me,' she grinned, and then she watched him transfer his equipment to his battered jeep which had stood partly hidden beyond the trees.

'Want a lift?' he asked, slanting a questioning glance at her when he slid his tall frame behind the wheel, and she shook her head.

'It's not far to walk, and after sitting for such a long time I certainly need the exercise.'

'Tomorrow, same time, same place, then?'

'I'll be here.'

She watched him drive away, the jeep bumping over the uneven track, and quite suddenly she experienced the strangest sense of loss. She tried to shake it off as she turned and stared a long way up at the waterfall, but instead she found herself wondering what this odd attraction was that she felt for Hammond Scott. He was good-looking, she supposed, in a rugged sort of way, and his kisses had certainly stirred something within her which she had never experienced before, but what was it about him that made him so different from other men? In her mother's eyes he had absolutely nothing to commend him. He was nothing but a poor, struggling artist, but that made no difference to Abbey. It was the man himself that mattered in some strange way, and she wished she could understand what was happening to her. Perhaps, as her mother had suggested, she was going quite mad.

Abbey met Hammond at the waterfall every morning for the rest of that week, and it was something she began to look forward to. He never kissed her again, but there was a growing awareness within her which she could not deny. His mere presence sparked off something inside her that was quite mysterious, and her pulses behaved most irrationally when he happened to touch her. Abbey wondered at times whether he was aware of the effect he had on her, but, if he was, then he never mentioned it, and she was spared the embarrassment of having to explain herself.

She went out riding early on the Saturday morning, taking Nomad on a stiff gallop across the veld, but instead of feeling exhilarated when she returned to the house, she felt curiously deflated on this occasion. She would not be meeting Hammond after breakfast that morning. They could give it a break over the weekend, he had said, and, not wanting to sound too eager, she had not contradicted his decision. She wished now that she had not kept silent, for the weekend loomed ahead of her rather drearily—unless, of course, she could think up an acceptable excuse to pay him a visit at his caravan.

'Don't be ridiculous!' her subconscious warned. 'You're thinking and behaving like a schoolgirl with a crush on her teacher. Looking for an excuse to visit him at his caravan, indeed! No self-respecting girl would go unchaperoned to a man's living quarters, and you know that!'

No self-respecting girl, her words echoed repeatedly and mockingly through her mind. She was beginning to think that she had no self-respect where Hammond Scott was concerned. She wanted to be with him, she wanted to hear him speak, she wanted to watch the sun turn his hair to burnished copper and, most of all, she longed to know again that wild elation she had experienced when he had kissed her.

Abbey shook herself free of these disturbing thoughts with an angry exclamation on her lips. She *was* going crazy. *Quite* crazy! She walked back to the house, her stride brisk and determined, and she was curiously breathless when she entered the house through the kitchen door. Her heart was beating heavily against her ribs, but she refused to believe that it was caused by anything other than the exertion. She *would* not believe it.

They were on the point of leaving the table after a late, leisurely breakfast that morning when the sound of an approaching car made Abbey and her father glance up at each other sharply.

'It seems as though we have visitors,' Edward remarked, glancing out of the breakfast-room window to catch a glimpse of the car, but he was unsuccessful.

'It's Derek,' Claire informed them without the slightest sign of guilt on her remarkably smooth features. 'I telephoned him during the week, and invited him to come and spend the weekend with us.'

'You did what?' Abbey almost screamed at her.

'How could you do such a thing, Claire?' Edward demanded almost at the same time.

'Abbey has had a week to come to her senses, and the rest is up to Derek,' Claire replied stubbornly, unmoved by her husband's fury.

'I'm going out,' Abbey snapped, pushing back her chair and leaping to her feet.

'No, you're not!' her mother's shrill, commanding voice raked along her nerves. 'You're going to see him, and you're going to give him the opportunity to talk a little sense into you.'

'Mother, I——'

'Good morning, everyone,' Derek's voice interrupted, and three pairs of eyes swivelled round to see him entering the room, but his dark glance went at once to the taut, slim figure of the girl who stood observing him coldly from the other end of the room. 'Hello, Abbey.'

'Hello, Derek,' she returned the greeting stiffly, making no further attempt to speak to him.

'Could I offer you a cup of tea, Derek?' Claire finally broke the awkward silence.

'That would be nice, thank you, Mrs Mitchell,' Derek smiled at her gratefully, pulling out a chair to join her at the table.

'You must have left Durban pretty early this morning,' Abbey's father remarked in an obvious effort to make civil conversation.

'I left at five o'clock, and the road was reasonably quiet,' Derek replied, stirring his tea and taking a mouthful before he added: 'My parents send their regards, by the way.'

'Thank you, my dear,' Claire flashed a smile at him, and once again there was that awkward silence which Abbey had neither the desire nor the inclination to break.

'I have work to do,' Edward muttered eventually, and he strode out of the room without so much as a second glance at Derek.

'And I have to see to things in the kitchen,' Claire announced, rising to her feet and casting a reproving glance at Abbey before she, too, walked out of the room.

Abbey remained rigidly on her feet until Derek had finished his tea, then he pushed away his cup and glanced up at her. 'Shall we go for a walk?'

Abbey almost laughed out loud. Derek, who disliked any form of physical exertion, was suggesting that they go for a walk, and she knew perfectly well that he hoped she would not accept his casual invitation.

'That's a good idea,' she agreed out of sheer devilment, and she did not miss the slight grimace that flashed across his handsome face as he pushed back his chair and got to his feet.

'Abbey, I've had a great deal of time to think this week, and you were right,' he said as they strolled across the lawn to a secluded section of the garden. 'I took a lot of things for granted, and——'

'Please, Derek.' She stopped in her stride and raised a hand in protest. 'If you're going to ask me to become engaged to you again, then the answer is "no". I've had a lot of time to think as well and, if I wasn't sure before, then I'm sure now. I can't ever marry you.'

His hand caught hold of hers and held it tightly. 'I love you, Abbey.'

'I'm sorry,' she whispered ruefully. 'I wish I could feel the same way about you, but I don't, and I realise now that I never did.'

'You're just being difficult,' he argued impatiently. 'Your mother says——'

'My mother says a lot of things to suit herself,' Abbey interrupted him, and she could barely keep the hostility out of her voice. 'She wants me to marry into a socially and financially secure family, and that's all that concerns her.'

Derek scowled down at her. 'How can you say things like that about your mother?'

'I can say them because they're true!' she snapped, jerking her hand from his. 'It's not my happiness she wants so desperately, it's the satisfaction of being able to say that her daughter married into the influential Halstead family that appeals to her.'

'What's so terrible about that?' he demanded haughtily.

'There's nothing terrible about it, but I'm not going to marry you merely to please my mother, Derek.' She gestured expressively with her hands and turned away from him when she saw the pain in his eyes. 'I'm sorry. You say you love me, and I believe you do, but I can't honestly say that my feelings for you are the same. I liked you very much, and I enjoyed your company, but that's not a sound basis for a marriage, and you must realise that as well.'

'Abbey . . .'

His hands were on her shoulders, but she shrugged them off and turned abruptly to face him. 'I think we've said all there is to be said on the subject.'

'But——'

'You're welcome to stay the weekend if you like,' she continued as if he had not spoken, 'but then it must be on the clear understanding that there can never be more than friendship between us.'

He stared at her incredulously for a moment, then he gestured angrily with his hands. 'You're asking the impossible!'

'Then it's up to you whether you go or stay,' she shrugged and, turning on her heel, she walked back to the house at a brisk pace.

To Abbey's relief, Derek left immediately after lunch, and when his car had disappeared down the drive she found herself confronted by her mother, who seemed barely able to contain her fury.

'You're just an obstinate, foolish child, Abigail, and I can only hope that there's still time for you to come to your senses,' she spat out the words viciously, then she swung round and disappeared into the house, leaving Abbey and her father alone in the driveway.

'Do what your heart tells you to do, Abbey,' her father said, placing his arm about her shoulders in a comforting gesture, then he turned away and, with his pipe clenched between his teeth, he followed her mother into the house.

By the set of his jaw Abbey knew that her parents were to have one of their rare arguments, and she deliberately walked away from the house, her steps taking her irrevocably towards Hammond's caravan.

The stream was running strong and swiftly when she crossed the low bridge fifteen minutes later and walked purposefully towards Hammond's camping site. His jeep was there, but there appeared to be no one about, and she wondered dismally whether he had gone off somewhere to sketch the scenery.

'Hammond?' she called tentatively. 'Hammond, are you there?'

There was no answer, but the caravan door stood open, and the temptation to go inside was too strong to ignore. Neat, compact, and spacious were the adjectives which came to mind when she stepped inside, but she could find no words to describe what she felt when she saw Hammond reclining on the double bunk at the far end of the caravan. He was lying on his back with his hands locked behind his head, and his eyes were grey-green slits of angry fire raking her from the top of her dark head down to her small, sandalled feet.

'Why didn't you answer when I called?' she managed shakily, determined not to be intimidated by him.

'I was hoping you'd think that I was out,' he replied harshly, and without the slightest concern for her feelings.

'I'm sorry,' she muttered apologetically, wincing

inwardly. 'I never realised I would be intruding on your privacy.'

'Don't be a damned idiot!' he barked at her when she turned to leave. 'I'm simply not in the mood to congratulate you a second time on your engagement.'

She turned to stare at him in surprise. 'How did you know that Derek was here?'

'Your father told me.'

'I see.' She swallowed nervously, and added a little sarcastically, 'I don't suppose my father has had time to tell you that Derek has left again?'

Hammond's eyes narrowed speculatively. 'He's not staying the weekend?'

'No,' she shook her head, 'and neither am I engaged to him again.'

'You're playing hard to get, are you?' he smiled cynically, reaching for the packet of cigarettes on the cupboard beside the bunk, and lighting one.

'I'm doing nothing of the kind,' she protested adamantly. 'I don't want to marry him, and I told him so.'

'Come here,' Hammond instructed when a few strained seconds had elapsed, and she obeyed instinctively, allowing him to take her hand and draw her down so that she was forced to sit on the bunk beside him. 'Do you know your own mind, I wonder?'

'I know that I could never marry him.'

'You're very sure.'

'Of course, I'm sure,' she insisted at once.

'You're very beautiful when you're angry,' he said, crushing his newly lit cigarette into the ashtray, and untying the bright red scarf that held her hair in place. 'Your eyes sparkle like deep blue sapphires, and——'

'Don't, Hammond,' she pleaded when he pushed his hands through her loosened hair, and caressed her throat with sensual fingers.

'Why not?' he smiled mockingly.

'You—you confuse me.'

'In what way?'

He trailed a lazy, tantalising finger down to the V of her blouse, and she was somehow powerless to stop him.

'I've never met anyone like you before.'

'Now what's that supposed to mean, I wonder?'

'It means that I shouldn't be alone here with you in your caravan,' she managed unsteadily, her pulse racing as she gripped his hand to prevent him from undoing the top button of her blouse.

'Are you afraid of me?' he mocked her, and her colour deepened.

'I—I think I'm more afraid of—of myself.'

'Your honesty is commendable,' he told her after a brief, astonished silence. 'Not many women would admit that they're afraid of their own feelings.'

'If I'm to survive, then I have to be honest,' she whispered, aware of something happening between them; something she could not control, and she fought it with honesty, the only weapon she had access to at that moment. 'I came here to you because I needed to talk to someone impartial; someone who could perhaps give me the sympathy and understanding I needed, but I know now that that's not quite the truth. I came simply because I wanted to be with you, and now I'm afraid. I'm afraid of you, I'm afraid of myself, and—and I think I should go.'

His hands snaked with lightning swiftness about her wrists, preventing her from getting to her feet, and those peculiar eyes held hers captive. 'Are you a coward, Abbey?'

'I—I don't think so,' she managed, conscious of his fingers resting against the tender skin where her pulse was beating much too hard and fast.

'You could run from me, but you can't run from yourself.'

That was true, she thought, although she might have no other alternative but to run from him, as well as herself.

'Are you suggesting that I should stay and face the music, so to speak?'

His fingers trailed a seductive path up her left arm, making her skin come alive responsively, then his hand was at the nape of her neck, and he was forcing her head relentlessly down towards his.

'I suggest you give yourself the opportunity of discovering exactly what you came here for.'

Her lustrous hair, like a black, silken veil, fell forward, and he worked his hands through it, the touch of his fingers making her scalp tingle. Her lips quivered in fearful anticipation as she stared down into his narrowed, mocking eyes, and she knew suddenly what it felt like to be a butterfly fluttering helplessly in the hands of its captor.

'Hammond . . .' she heard herself protest weakly, but his mouth was already sliding over hers to silence her in a devastatingly effective way.

She responded with an eagerness she would no doubt be ashamed of later, and she felt his heavy heartbeats quicken beneath her hands moments before he pulled her down beside him, and reversed their positions. Trapped beneath the hard length of his muscular body, she knew a moment of panic, but his lips teased and provoked until, with a curious little moan, she drew his head down to deepen their kiss. This time, when he undid the buttons of her blouse, she offered no protest, and the touch of his hands against her responsive flesh sent a shiver of sensual excitement rippling through her. His teeth nibbled playfully at her earlobe, sending the most primitive sensations cascading through her, and she was no longer in a position to stop him when he undid the front catch of her bra.

Her breasts swelled to the unfamiliar touch of a man's hands, and the tantalising caress of those sensitive fingers aroused emotions which were totally alien to her. She tried to think coherently, but she couldn't, and when his warm, sensually arousing mouth followed the exploratory path of his hands, she experienced a powerful surge of emotion that drove her to a peak of desire which was frightening in its intensity. She trembled with the force of it, and Hammond instantly moulded her to him, making her achingly aware of his as well as her own need, but she stirred in an unconscious protest beneath him when his hand strayed to the fastening of her slacks.

Hammond did not remove his hand, and neither did he pursue his efforts, but his expression was faintly mocking when he raised his head and found her unaware of the fact that her eyes had darkened considerably with the extent of her emotions.

'This—this isn't something new to you, is it?' she said unsteadily, recognising the signs of a man who was not accustomed to exercising such a rigid control where his desires were concerned.

'No,' he admitted with a hint of amusement hovering about his mouth.

'Have there been many women?' she persisted, not quite knowing why she should want to punish herself in this painful way.

'A man of integrity never speaks of his conquests.'

Abbey considered this for a moment before she said haltingly, 'I don't think I—I want to be added to the list of your conquests, Hammond.'

His mouth twisted cruelly. 'I never suggested it, did I?'

'No,' she admitted truthfully, dragging the front of her blouse together with shaking hands when she realised that she was allowing him to see far too much of her anatomy, then she said coldly, 'Let me get up, please.'

Hammond rolled away from her at once, and swung his long legs off the bunk. That left her plenty of room to scramble off on to the floor, and he at least had the decency to turn his back while she frantically restored a certain amount of order to her appearance.

'Abbey . . .'

'Don't touch me!' she cried hoarsely, cringing away from him when he came near her. 'I—I'm ashamed of myself.'

'You have no reason to be ashamed.'

'Oh, yes, I have,' she argued jerkily as she swung round to face him. 'I—I've never before allowed any man to touch me the way you have—and, no matter what you think of me, that's the truth.'

'I believe you.'

'Thank you,' she murmured, still unable to raise her glance higher than the opening of his shirt.

'Look at me,' he ordered harshly, and when she refused to obey, he cupped her chin in his hand and forced her to meet his compelling eyes. 'This started out as a session of honesty, and it might as well continue along those lines. Your innocence couldn't have prevented you from guessing how much I wanted you a moment ago, and I'm not ashamed to admit it. You're a very beautiful and desirable young woman, but you still have a lot to learn. Your body is not something to be ashamed of. It was designed to give and receive pleasure, and if you deny the enjoyment you experienced, then you certainly have something to be ashamed of.' His eyes challenged her. 'Do you deny it?'

'No!' she whispered hoarsely. 'No, I don't!'

Without warning, she was caught up against him, her small softness crushed against the hard length of him, and his kiss, although bruising, still had the power to stir the blood in her veins until she felt quite intoxicated. Her hands went up to his shoulders, clinging to their muscled hardness as a weakness invaded her limbs, and when he finally released her she was shaking and swaying helplessly on her feet.

'I think I should go,' she said jerkily, clutching at the cupboard behind her for support until her legs became steadier.

'I think so too,' he smiled twistedly. 'I'll see you on Monday morning at eighty-thirty.'

Abbey was never quite sure how she managed to get back to the house. Her heart was drumming so hard and fast in her ears that she thought it would never stop, and her legs felt like two rubberised objects unwilling to do her bidding.

The house was silent when she entered, and she went straight to her room, wanting to be alone and undisturbed while she sorted out the turmoil in her mind and heart. What had happened that afternoon in Hammond's caravan was something which still had the power to make her blush. She had allowed him intimacies she had never allowed anyone else before, and he had aroused emotions which she would never have thought herself capable of. It had been madness; an intoxicating madness, and she had so very nearly cast aside the principles which she had always lived up to. It would have been so incredibly easy to surrender herself to Hammond; she had, in fact, been on the verge of it, and it was this thought which frightened her most of all.

'What's happening to me?' she wondered frantically.

Was this merely a physical reaction, or was there something more to it? Whatever it was, she decided at length, it had been like receiving a stunning blow without quite knowing where it had come from.

She barely knew the man, and yet it felt as if she had known him all her life. In a matter of a few days he had become an inseparable part of her existence; a necessary and vital part, and the mere thought of him eventually walking out of her life filled her with such a feeling of dreaded desolation that she wanted to rush back to his caravan to beg him never to leave her. If this was not madness, then what was? she wondered a little cynically.

That evening, when she sat alone on the terrace with her father, Abbey said hesitantly, 'There's something—something very serious I need to discuss with you.'

Her father re-lit his pipe, and in the light of the match she could see him smiling at her encouragingly. 'It's quite like old times, isn't it?'

'Yes, it is,' she nodded, realising that it was a long time indeed since she had felt the need to confide in her father, or to ask his advice about something personal.

'I realised at the dinner table this evening that something was troubling you,' he remarked shrewdly, blowing out the match and dropping it into the ashtray beside him. 'What's the problem?'

Abbey stared at his dark shape in the chair close to hers, and inhaled the familiar aroma of his pipe tobacco as it mingled with the scent of the night flowers. She did not quite know where to begin, but she had to make a start somewhere, even if she had to work her way backwards through it.

'What does it mean?' she began at last. 'What does it mean when you find that you want to spend every available moment with someone, even if it's just to look at them, or to listen to their voice?'

'Is there someone specific who's making you feel this way?'

'Yes, there is.'

'Hammond Scott?'

Abbey drew a sharp, startled breath. 'How did you know?'

'It was a wild guess, nothing more.'

'Dad, I don't know what's the matter with me,' she groaned. 'When I'm away from him I can't seem to get him out of my mind, and when I'm with him I—I feel anything but contented. I'm like a tightly coiled spring needing release, and finding none.'

'You've never felt like this before?'

She shook her head helplessly. 'No.'

'I would say you have a bad dose of that virus called love,' her father remarked casually, but his words travelled like shockwaves along her nerves.

'Love?' she whispered, shrinking inwardly from the word. 'Oh, no, I don't . . .'

'Don't you?' her father prompted when her voice trailed off into silence.

'But I barely know him!' she protested, her hands clutching at the arms of her chair in an effort to stop them from shaking.

'Time is of no essence where love is concerned,' Edward informed her drily. 'The first time I met your mother I knew that I loved her, and wanted to marry her.'

'But what I feel is such a physical thing,' she argued, incapable at that moment of accepting her father's startling suggestion.

'Love *is* a physical thing,' Edward reminded her a little mockingly. 'Love is not merely wanting to be with someone, it's wanting to be with them in mind, body, and spirit. There's only one way to show one's love, and that's physically, so don't exclude the physical side of it as if it were of no consequence.' He knocked out his pipe in the ashtray and leaned forward in his chair in a confidential manner. 'The physical side of loving someone is not something one starts thinking of only after the marriage ceremony. It's something you think about long before that wedding ring is placed on your finger.'

'Men don't always make love to women because they love them,' Abbey heard herself arguing.

'That's true,' her father admitted. 'A man's desire is very easily aroused, and he could take a woman out of pure lust, but when he loves the woman then his desire takes on a completely different dimension.'

'How can you be sure, then, that what you feel is not pure lust?'

'Lust is something you feel for someone whom you could walk away from tomorrow without the slightest feeling of regret.' There was a brief silence filled only by the sounds of the insects in the undergrowth, then her father asked quietly, 'Is that how you feel about him?'

'No!' The word came out softly, but decisively. 'I could never walk away from him, and not care whether I saw him again or not.'

'Then I think you have your answer.'

She stared at her father's dark shape for interminable seconds, then a new anxiety gripped her insides. 'You won't tell anyone, will you, Dad?'

They both knew that she was referring specifically to her mother, and Edward stated firmly, 'I have never yet divulged one fragment of our private conversations.'

'Thank you,' she whispered, leaning forward impulsively to kiss him on his rough cheek, and she left him there a few minutes later to return to her room.

There was no joy in the knowledge that she loved Hammond, only a gnawing anxiety, and a fear far greater than anything she had known before. What if he did not care for her in return? He had said that she was beautiful, and he had made love to her a little, but that did not mean that he loved her. Hammond had known many women, she was certain of that, and she had no doubt that they had come and gone out of his life without him feeling the slightest regret. Why, then, should he feel any different about her?

CHAPTER SIX

THE clouds built up on the Sunday, and it rained during the night in a steady downpour which continued throughout the next two days, making it impossible for Abbey to meet Hammond at the usual place. On the Monday morning she had put on her raincoat and had taken a walk down to his caravan, but she had found it locked, and the jeep had gone. On the Tuesday morning she found that nothing had altered, and there were no fresh tracks in the muddy ground to indicate that he had been there at all since the day before.

On both occasions Abbey had returned to the house feeling miserable and wet, and it was with an audible sigh of relief that she watched the sun break through the clouds late on the Tuesday afternoon. The stars were brilliant in the sky that night, promising a long, hot day to follow after the rain, and it was with a sense of elation that she left the house on the Wednesday morning to make her way towards the waterfall.

Hammond was there, leaning casually against a tree

and smoking a cigarette as he so often did when he had to wait for her. His eyes were narrowed in his rugged face, giving her no indication what he was thinking, and she approached him rather hesitantly. It was not until she was almost within touching distance of him that he spoke, and her nerve-ends quivered at the harsh note in his voice.

'You're late,' he said abruptly, his eyes raking her accusingly.

'I wasn't sure whether you would be here or not.'

'Why wouldn't I be here?' he demanded, flinging his cigarette to the ground and crushing it beneath the heel of his canvas shoe. 'The sun is shining, and the light is absolutely perfect.'

'You weren't at your caravan yesterday, and neither were you there the day before.'

'It was raining, and I had business elsewhere to attend to.' His smile was instantly mocking. 'Did you miss me?'

'Would it flatter your ego if I said yes?'

'I'm not asking for flattery,' he replied curtly, and his potent masculinity held her motionless as he cupped her chin in his hand and raised her face to his. 'A simple yes or no would do.'

'Yes,' she heard herself admitting a little breathlessly, unable to wrench her eyes from his. 'I missed you.'

For a moment he did not react, then his hands slid beneath her hair and, filling his clenched fists with its silky lustre, he lowered his mouth to hers and parted her lips with an expertise that sent a thrill of exquisite excitement surging into her very marrow. It was a lingering kiss, sensual and explorative, and a shiver of emotion rippled through her when his hands slid possessively down her back. Her hips and thighs became moulded to his, making her intensely aware of his maleness, and of a need that sent an unfamiliar ache surging from the lower half of her body down into her limbs, and a little sigh escaped her as she raised her arms and locked them about his neck in an unconscious effort to get closer to him.

'If we start the morning in this manner, then I'm never going to complete your portrait,' he said at length, nibbling at her ear and sending delicious little shivers racing up and down her spine. 'You're a very distracting little witch.'

'Hammond?' she began, drawing away from him slightly to glance up at him questioningly.

'Sit down over there and behave yourself,' he instructed, his manner changing abruptly as he disengaged himself from her, and her heart was still pounding wildly when she obeyed him. 'Relax, and don't fidget,' he ordered when she tried to settle down to the routine they had followed the week before.

'I'm sorry,' she gulped, but it was almost impossible trying to relax when she was aware of him with every quivering nerve in her body.

She loved him; she knew that now without doubt, and if he were truly a penniless tramp she could not love him less. She would follow him to the ends of the earth if he would but ask her to, and it was this startling truth that made her realise the full extent of her feelings for this man.

The faint smell of oils and turps lingered in the air that morning as he worked on in siilence, and Abbey did not disturb him with idle chatter. She was, in fact, too emotionally disturbed to think of anything to say. It was a hot day, and the scorching rays of the sun on the damp earth culminated in creating a humidity which sent the perspiration trickling uncomfortably down the hollow of Abbey's back. Her cotton blouse finally clung limply to her body, and the stiffness in her back spread slowly into her legs until they felt numb. She wanted desperately to alter her position, but she dared not, so she simply sat there staring at the clear, rippling water, and wished that she could fling herself into its cool depths for just a few minutes.

'That's enough for today,' Hammond said at last, and she was carefully arching her back and stretching out her legs when he joined her there on the rock. From the top pocket of his blue checked shirt he brought out a squashed packet of cigarettes, and she watched him unobtrusively while he lit one. He smoked in silence for a while, and she marvelled at the thickness of his lashes, but she looked away hastily when he turned his head abruptly to glance at her. 'That water looks inviting,' he echoed her own thoughts of a few minutes ago.

'It does,' she murmured, risking a second glance at him, and saw the question in his eyes before he spoke.

'Shall we?'

'I haven't a swimsuit here with me,' she told him regretfully.

'Neither have I.' His eyes mocked her when he heard her draw her breath in sharply, but before she could recover from the shock of his unspoken suggestion, he said: 'You may go in first, if you like.'

'While you sit here and watch me?' she asked in astonishment.

A cynical smile curved his mouth. 'I'll be a gentleman, for once, and turn my back.'

Abbey stared at him contemplatively. Many times in the past she had yielded to the temptation, and had dived into these clear waters without a stitch of clothing on, but on those occasions she had been alone. This time Hammond would be there, and although she knew the dangers involved, the temptation to submerge herself in the pool's refreshing water finally motivated her decision.

'Turn around,' she said quickly before she could change her mind, and her cheeks reddened with embarrassment when she glimpsed that split-second mockery in his eyes before he turned his back on her.

She stripped as quickly as her trembling hands would allow her, and the heat of the sun was on her naked body but a few brief seconds before she plunged into the water to emerge in the centre where it was at its deepest.

'Now it's your turn,' she shouted above the gushing roar of the waterfall. 'And you're to keep your distance!'

'My dear Abbey,' Hammond laughed, and she shrank further beneath the water when he turned to face her, 'you wouldn't be the first woman I've seen without her clothes on.'

Her hands went instinctively to her breasts, and her voice was an unsteady squeak when she said: 'I don't doubt that, but I still insist that you keep your distance.'

'If you say so,' he shrugged, unbuttoning his shirt and flinging it on to the rock where they had sat.

The muscles rippled in his tanned chest and arms as he pulled off his shoes, but, when his hands went to the buckle of his belt, she realised with something close to horror that she had been staring and, worse still, that Hammond had no intention of turning his back on her while he stripped off his clothes. She twirled round in the water, and swam towards the other side of the pool with leisurely strokes, making a desperate attempt to appear casual and unconcerned, but her heart was beating much too fast, and her body was taut with nerves as she waited for him to join her in the pool.

Her nerves reacted sharply at the sound of him diving into the water, and moments later she realised that she had had every reason to be nervous and edgy. He was swimming towards her with long, powerful strokes, and she was going hot and cold at the horrifying realisation that the water was much too clear for comfort. She had been a crazy, idiotic fool to allow herself to be tempted into this situation, and fear drummed loudly in her ears as she frantically tried to put some distance between them.

'Hammond!' she shrieked at length when she realised that he was gaining on her. 'Stay away from me, do you hear!' Strong white teeth flashed in his tanned, rugged face and, as she thrashed out with her legs in yet another desperate attempt to put some distance between them, steel-like fingers latched on to her ankle, and she was pulled towards him relentlessly.

'No, Hammond! *No!*' she begged, a note of panic in her voice, but her thrashing arms were caught smartly at the wrists, and she was pulled towards him until their bodies almost touched.

'You're beautiful, Abbey,' he said softly, his eyes probing the whiteness of her slender body beneath the water, then he raised his glance to her full, quivering lips.

Her heart was beating in her mouth, and a shyness and fear combined to blind her to the unexpected tenderness in his gaze as she begged hoarsely, 'Please ... let me go!'

'Don't be afraid,' he murmured, and then his cool, wet mouth took command of hers.

She remained passive, hoping desperately that he would soon set her free, but she had not taken into account that her treacherous emotions might betray her. Her lips parted beneath the sensual pressure of his, and a wild, sweet emotion stirred within her when his hands freed her wrists to encircle her waist. His knees knocked against hers as they trod water automatically, then she was drawn into a closer embrace until their bodies touched and became fused together. Unfamiliar sensations swamped her at the muscled hardness of a man's naked body against her own. She knew a moment of panic, the rigid principles by which she had always lived flashing through her mind and issuing a frantic warning, but her body seemed to have a will of its own, and she melted against Hammond, surrendering to the demand of his lips and hands. His shoulders were cool and slippery beneath her fingers as she clung to him, and he did not release her as they went down into the darkened depths of the water.

Abbey was no longer afraid and, discarding her inhibitions, she locked her arms about his strong neck. His legs moved against hers, the movement bringing them up to the surface once more, and they drew breath simultaneously before they kissed again with a passionate intensity as they sank beneath the water a second time.

He released her at last, and they kicked themselves up to the surface. In the grip of something far stronger than she had ever before experienced, she lost her shyness, and they swam together, diving and twirling about in the water as children might have done. There was a difference, though. Hammond was potently male, and she was a woman who had never been more aware of her own femininity. It was a totally new experience, knowing that she had the power to entice a man with her body and, unintentionally, they played the seductive game of the hunted and the hunter. She remained elusive, her laughter echoing across the water as she twisted and darted beyond his reach, but Hammond remained her superior. He captured her several times, and she was powerless to resist as he caressed her beneath the water, his hands sliding over her body in a way which awakened the most primitive emotions, then he would allow her to twist beyond his reach, and the chase would start again. She was playing with fire, she knew it, but for some strange reason she did not care.

Abbey should have looked the other way when Hammond eventually climbed out of the pool, but she found herself observing him unashamedly. His wet, gleaming body was muscled and tanned evenly as if swimming naked was something he often indulged in, and, for the first time in her life, she realised that a man's body could be beautiful. The muscles rippled beneath the smooth skin, and recalling the feel of his body against her own was enough to send the blood running swiftly and urgently through her veins.

She sensed that Hammond was aware of her scrutiny, but he did not seem to care. As she had sensed his awareness of her glance, so he must have sensed the shyness which she could not quite eradicate, and he turned his back on her in silence while she climbed out of the pool and pulled her clothes on to her wet body. She wrung her hair out between her hands and, when she flicked it over her shoulder, Hammond was standing directly in front of her, his feet apart, and his eyes narrowed against the sun. She felt certain that she looked a mess, but his hands were hard and firm on her shoulders before she could move away, and she had a blurred vision of his ruggedly handsome face before his mouth fastened on to hers.

There was no room for thought in her mind, and her legs simply seemed to give way beneath her. He followed her down on to the soft grass, and his broad shoulders shut out the sun as he moulded her body to his and kissed her with a mounting passion that seared through her like a flame intent upon scorching her soul. A wild desire throbbed through her veins until every nerve and sinew in her body was aware of his weight above her, and she was aching for his touch long before his fingers undid the buttons of her blouse and snapped the catch of her bra. A shudder of emotion shook through her when his hand cupped her breast, and while those clever fingers probed and caressed, his lips left hers to trail a path of fiery delight along her smooth throat towards one cool, exposed shoulder. She moaned softly, partly in protest and partly in pleasure, but she could no longer control the fierce desire that clamoured through her when his warm, tantalising lips expanded their exploration across the swell of her breast.

'Hammond . . .' she breathed his name almost reverently, and then, in that moment of intense emotion, she could not curb those revealing words which hovered on her lips. 'Hammond,' she whispered, her fingers working their way almost feverishly through his hair. 'I love you, Hammond.'

She heard her voice as if from a distance and, dismayed at having confessed her feelings, she waited with bated breath for Hammond's reaction. Would he laugh at her, or would he simply reject her? she wondered frantically.

He did neither; he merely raised his head and, with a faint smile lifting the corners of his mouth, he asked: 'Do you?'

It was a casual question, but not the kind that warranted a reply, and it was with a certain amount of relief that she drew his head down to hers, seeking his mouth with her own, and giving him a wordless confirmation to his query—if he cared to accept it.

The magical moment ended all too soon, and Abbey

felt lost and curiously deflated when Hammond released her and got to his feet. He walked away from her while she fastened the catch of her bra and buttoned up her blouse with shaking hands, and her fingers fumbled a little as she watched him pack away his paints and fold up his easel. He looked oddly remote, almost as if he were unaware of her presence, and it hurt intensely when she sensed that she was being shut out of his life. She wanted to share his thoughts, and she wanted to be a part of his dreams, but she had a horrible suspicion that her having voiced her feelings, in that unguarded moment, was the cause of this impregnable wall of silence between them.

'I'm taking a drive in to Bergville this afternoon,' she said in sheer desperation to break this awful silence, and her throat felt curiously dry as she accompanied him to his jeep. 'Is there anything you need?' she asked, making an attempt to behave as if nothing had happened.

He glanced at her then, but his grey-green eyes were painfully impersonal. 'You could check at the hotel if any post has arrived for me.'

'I'll do that,' she nodded absently, shifting her weight uncomfortably from one foot on to the other like a nervous child. 'Nothing else?'

His eyes mocked her for some reason, plunging her mind into a state of confusion, and flooding her cheeks with a humiliating warmth as his glance travelled slowly down the length of her body, making several detours in the process as if he were savouring in his mind those moments they had shared in and out of the water.

'I need nothing except this,' he said at length, jerking her up against him with unexpected swiftness to engage her mouth with his.

Abbey's pulses were clamouring, and her lips were throbbing with the fierceness of his kiss when she watched him drive away moments later. Instead of feeling elated, she felt miserable, and all at once incredibly lonely. She was shivering despite the heat of the sun, and something, a premonition perhaps, flashed through her mind. It was an elusive image which she did not wish to dwell on, but she could not quite succeed in her attempts to wipe out that vision of an emptiness that loomed ahead of her. She was being silly, she told herself, but that awful feeling persisted. Something was going to happen. She sensed it, and it frightened her.

It did not take Abbey very long to purchase the few items on her list, and it was when she was on her way out of town that she stopped at the hotel. After a brief enquiry at the reception desk, she was handed a large white envelope, and it bulged with its contents. In the car, before driving away, Abbey inspected the envelope curiously, turning it over several times in her agitated hands. The handwriting looked feminine, but the name on the back of the envelope gave nothing away. 'S. Varney,' she read out aloud, and a post-office box number in Johannesburg followed.

Perhaps it had something to do with the exhibition he was planning, she consoled herself and, placing the envelope on the seat beside her, she drove back to Sweet Waters.

When she arrived at Hammond's caravan that afternoon she found him sitting on a canvas chair while he sorted through a pile of sketches, and he looked up only briefly when she approached him.

'I've brought your post,' she said unnecessarily, knowing that he could not have missed the large, bulky envelope in her hands.

'Thank you,' he nodded, taking it from her, and flinging it unceremoniously into a vacant chair.

'The handwriting looks feminine,' she voiced her suspicions, hating herself for prying into his affairs, but unable to prevent herself from doing so.

'It *is* feminine.'

'What does the "S" stand for?'

'Shelagh,' he supplied the answer abruptly.

Abbey went rigid as she observed the concentration with which he was examining his sketches, then she asked bluntly, 'Do you care for her?'

'In a manner of speaking, yes.'

'Oh!' she managed in a choked voice as a searing stab of unfamiliar jealousy shot straight through her heart.

Hammond looked up then, his face dispassionate and his eyes shuttered as he gestured towards the flask standing on the fold-up table. 'Want some coffee?'

She turned away from him abruptly, afraid of what he might see in her eyes. 'No, thank you.'

'Abbey?'

He was behind her in an instant, his fingers biting into her shoulders as he swung her round to face him, and she went into his arms with a despicable eagerness, her hands sliding up across his broad back towards his shoulders as she felt herself drowning in his fiery kisses.

'There are times when I think I don't like you at all,' she said, a note of anger in her voice when, at last, she was given the opportunity to breathe freely, but his lips were exploring her creamy shoulder where his impatient fingers had brushed aside the narrow strap of her sundress, and the touch of his warm mouth against her flesh sent a shiver of primitive emotion cascading through her.

She wanted this moment to go on for ever, but all too soon he thrust her aside and said sternly, 'If you don't want coffee, then I suggest you go home, but I want you here at eighty-thirty tomorrow—if the weather lasts.'

'Here?' she asked incredulously, staring a long way up at him.

'I've done all the preliminaries. It's your face I need to concentrate on, and for that we don't need the enchanted waters of the dragon's pool,' he told her with a gleam of mockery in his eyes that sent a wave of colour surging into her cheeks.

'I'll see you tomorrow, then,' she said, her lips stiff with embarrassment as she turned and walked away from him.

She did not look back, she was determined not to, but she was intensely conscious of his eyes following her across the low bridge towards the opposite side of the stream where she knew that the low-hanging branches of the willow trees would hide her from his view.

A new anxiety was shaping in her mind in the form of Shelagh Varney. Who was she, and what was she to Hammond? He cared for her, he had said so, but what exactly did that mean? Did he love her, or was she merely his mistress?

Stabbing, painful thoughts were flinging her into a mire of uncertainty. They had shared something at Dragon's Cove that morning; something indescribably beautiful. Had it meant as much to him as it had meant to her, or had she merely joined the ranks of all those other women who had bared their souls as well as their bodies under his sensually persuasive influence? It was an agonisingly disturbing thought, and one that made her cringe inwardly with a fiery shame as she recalled how easily she had shed her clothes along with her inhibitions. Her confidence, at the time, had been born of her love for him, but her confidence had long since deserted her to leave her bewildered and unsure of herself.

At the dinner table that evening it was Abbey and her father who kept the conversation flowing. Claire had been strangely reticent since Derek's brief visit, keeping her opinions to herself, and speaking only when it was absolutely necessary. Abbey sensed, however, that something was brewing, and she shuddered to think what her mother would say if she should discover that her daughter had fallen in love with a penniless artist who was apparently of no fixed abode. She could quite imagine her mother's outrageous remarks, and a much-needed thread of humour wound its way through her anxious thoughts.

Abbey slept rather badly that night and, as a result, she was exhausted long before her lengthy session with Hammond ended the following morning, but she sat there without complaining until her shoulders and the back of her neck were aching.

'Tired?' Hammond asked at the very moment she decided that she could not take it a minute longer, and she nodded with a grimace. He put down his brushes and, much to her surprise, came up behind her and gently massaged her neck and shoulders, easing out the pain and relaxing the taut muscles in the process. 'Does that feel better?'

'Hm ... yes,' she murmured, closing her eyes and enjoying the touch of those strong hands which were beginning to arouse pleasurable sensations that had nothing to do with massaging her tired shoulders.

She leaned back against him and felt him stiffen, but before she could guess his intentions his hands tightened on her shoulders, and she was lifted almost bodily off the stool as he dragged her up into his arms. Her breasts hurt against his chest while his mouth invaded hers with an intimacy she was fast becoming familiar with, and her senses soared to those unimaginable heights before he eventually released her.

'Do you know how to use a gas stove?' he asked as she stood dazed and shaken before him.

'Yes,' she nodded, not quite ready for the swift descension from that heady cloud.

'Then I suggest you make us some coffee,' he instructed, and she could almost hate him for his disgusting calmness while she was still struggling with the feeling that her emotions had become scattered like fallen leaves in the wind. 'You'll find everything you need in the cupboard beneath the stove,' he added, giving her a gentle push in the general direction of the caravan, 'and there's fresh milk in the refrigerator.'

Abbey did as she was told, but she did so almost without thinking, and some minutes later she emerged from the caravan with a steaming mug of coffee in each hand.

'When will the portrait be finished?' she asked when she had seated herself beside him on a canvas chair, and she saw him shrug his wide shoulders in a way that made her aware of their muscled strength.

'Next week, I hope.'

'I must confess that I'm terribly anxious to see it.'

'You'll see it all in good time.' His eyes met hers across the rim of his mug, and his glance was curiously intent. 'Have you heard from Derek again lately?'

'No.' She shook her head and stared at him in surprise. 'Why do you ask?'

'I merely wondered,' he replied, his expression conveying nothing except a casual interest which bordered on indifference.

An involuntary sigh escaped her and, staring out across the fast-moving stream, she said quietly, 'I don't expect I shall see him again.'

'You sound rather sad about it.'

'If I sound sad, then it's because I . . .'

'Because you still care for him?' Hammond supplemented when she paused absently.

'In a way, yes,' she confessed. 'I *was* fond of him, and I know that I've hurt him.'

'You must have been more than fond of him to have considered marrying him,' Hammond suggested with a hint of cynicism in his voice.

'I thought I loved him,' she corrected with inherent honesty.

'What makes you think that you didn't?'

Abbey glanced at him sharply, and frowned. 'I know I didn't.'

'Are you sure?' he smiled twistedly.

'Of course I'm sure.' The atmosphere suddenly crackled with tension, and she heard herself laugh nervously. 'Hey, what is this? Why all these questions about my feelings for Derek?'

Hammond drained his mug and placed it on the grass beside his chair, then he looked up, and his eyes were a cold grey as they pinned her mercilessly to her seat. 'I don't think you know your own mind.'

Startled, she asked: 'What makes you think that?'

'Women seldom know their own minds,' he observed cynically. 'They imagine themselves in love one minute, and the next they're swooning over someone else.'

Resentment and anger surged through her, making her say stiffly, 'I suggest we change the subject.'

'Why?' he demanded bluntly. 'Does the truth hurt?'

'You're beginning to annoy me,' she warned, putting down her own mug and rising agitatedly to her feet.

'Don't you like being able to see yourself through someone else's eyes?' he mocked her ruthlessly, and her lashes fluttered down to veil the pain in her eyes when she turned to face him.

'Is that how you see me?' she asked, forcing the words past unwilling lips. 'A mindless butterfly flitting from one man to the next in search of excitement?'

'I have nothing but excitement to offer you, Abbey, but with Derek it was no doubt his position in society and his wealth that attracted you,' he stated with a harsh cynicism that cut her to the core. 'What will attract you next, I wonder?'

White with anger, she said coldly, 'At this moment your face is attracting the flat of my hand.'

'If it will relieve your frustration, then I suggest you go ahead,' he laughed infuriatingly, but when she turned from him abruptly and walked away, he demanded sharply, 'Where do you think you're going?'

'Home,' she announced firmly without pausing in her furious stride.

'Oh, no, you're not,' Hammond announced, moving with incredible speed to grip her wrist and swing her round to face him.

'Oh, yes, I am!' she protested fiercely, her eyes blazing up at him. 'I won't stay here and listen to more of your——'

His mouth silenced the rest of her tirade, and her attempts to escape his punishing kiss were thwarted when his hand became tangled in the hair at the nape of her neck. The punishment was brief but sufficient until, with a sensual expertise, he turned her limbs to water, and drew a response from her that sent the blood pounding madly through her veins.

'You don't really want to go, do you?' he asked against her lips, tantalising her with feather-like kisses.

'I'd rather go than continue this silly argument with you.'

'Were we arguing?' he questioned mockingly, drawing

away from her, and leaving her swaying on her feet with the aching need to be held in his arms a moment longer.

'You were saying the most dreadful things,' Abbey reminded him crossly, and his eyebrows rose with sardonic amusement.

'But I'm a dreadful man, didn't you know that?'

'Be serious, Hammond,' she pleaded desperately, 'and be as honest with me as I've been with you.'

The breeze lifted a silky curl across her flushed cheek, and he brushed it away with a lazy finger, tugging playfully as he did so, but there was nothing playful in those peculiar eyes probing her so intently. 'Have you been honest with me?'

'Haven't I been brazen enough to tell you that I love you?' she asked, shedding the remnants of her pride, but he remained unmoved.

'In a moment of passion a woman may say any number of things, none of them necessarily true.'

'What do I have to do to convince you?'

'Stay with me tonight.'

Her breath stilled momentarily in her throat. 'Would that convince you?'

'It might.'

'You sound doubtful,' she whispered unsteadily, her eyes searching desperately for some sign that he cared, but she searched in vain, and his twisted, cynical smile did not waver for an instant.

'There's always the possibility that I might need convincing more than once,' he replied casually.

'You don't really want to be convinced of anything,' she accused sharply, jerking her hair free of his fingers and stepping a pace away from him. 'All you're angling for is an affair.'

'You're right, of course,' he mocked her cruelly. 'I find it lonely out here at night.'

The playful breeze lifted her hair across her face once more, and she brushed it away impatiently as she flashed him a wounded, angry glance. 'You're laughing at me!'

'You must admit that there's an amusing side to the situation.'

'Yes, I suppose there is,' she agreed, fighting back the helpless tears. 'But the humour escapes me at the moment.'

'Abbey,' he sighed exasperatedly, 'do you know what your problem is?'

'What?'

'You take life much too seriously.'

'And you don't, I suppose,' she flung at him angrily.

'I can't afford to take women seriously,' he explained with annoying tolerance. 'No woman would be satisfied to live the kind of life I enjoy.'

'I would,' the words sprang to her lips, but she bit them back hastily, and said instead, 'If she loved you she would.'

'That's sentimental trash, and you know it,' Hammond gestured angrily. 'Women want security, a home, and children, and if a man can't give her that, then she goes out in search of it elsewhere.'

Abbey stared up at him helplessly for a moment, then she shook her head and gestured despairingly. 'I'm not going to argue with you.'

'That's good,' he said abruptly, 'because I want to get on with this portrait.'

Abbey resumed her seat on the stool with a certain reluctance, and the session continued for almost an hour before she was free to go, but their conversation churned relentlessly through her mind as she walked home that day, and it continued to do so until she was certain that she had never felt more miserable.

She could not have told Hammond more plainly what

she felt for him, and yet he remained aloof, mocking her emotions, and doubting her sincerity. Only time, perhaps, would convince him, but it was worrying not to know how much time they would actually have together.

CHAPTER SEVEN

ABBEY was entering the breakfast room on the Friday morning when she caught a glimpse of a car disappearing down the drive, and it was something more than curiosity that made her hasten towards the window, but she was a fraction too late to identify their early morning visitor.

'Who was that?' she questioned her mother when she entered the room moments later.

'She said her name was Shelagh Varney, and she was looking for Mr Scott,' Claire announced, seating herself at the table.

Abbey stared thoughtfully at her mother, and a strange tension coiled through her. 'Did you direct her to his caravan?'

'Naturally,' Claire smiled, and for some reason Abbey suspected that her mother was enjoying her discomfort.

She joined Claire at the table, but she could not conjure up her usual appetite, and settled for coffee instead. Shelagh Varney had come to Sweet Waters to see Hammond, and Abbey's mind was churning up all sorts of painful images. What was she doing here? Did Hammond know that she would be coming? Abbey tried not to think about it, but her mind gave her no peace.

Determined to meet this woman, she left the house at the usual time and walked down towards the stream where Hammond's caravan was parked, and the first thing she saw when she crossed the low bridge was the expensive-looking Mercedes parked in the shade of a willow tree close to the caravan. Whoever this Shelagh Varney was, Abbey decided, it was obvious that she was wealthy.

Abbey walked on, but with every step her nerves became more securely knotted in the pit of her stomach. She was not sure what she had expected, but when she approached Hammond's camping site she glimpsed a pair of shapely legs which obviously belonged to Shelagh Varney, and that was enough to set Abbey's teeth on edge. The rest of Hammond's visitor was obscured by his large bulk where he stood with his back turned towards Abbey.

Her foot accidentally kicked against a pebble, and Hammond swung round with a look of agitation on his face that made Abbey squirm with the awful feeling that she was intruding.

'Hello, Abbey.'

His voice was cool and impersonal, and Abbey sensed his displeasure as her glance darted towards the woman seated on the most comfortable canvas chair.

Shelagh Varney was blonde and beautiful, and her pale blue cotton suit had most certainly not been bought off the peg. She possessed an undeniable air of sophistication and elegance, and her clear brown eyes reflected an above-average intelligence which could not be disputed.

'Mother told me you had a visitor,' Abbey said, her mouth dry, and a sinking feeling in her chest as she allowed her glance to slide from Shelagh Varney towards Hammond who stood rigidly beside her chair.

'I'd like you to meet Shelagh Varney. She's a . . . a very good friend of mine,' Hammond announced, and that slight pause in his voice did not go unnoticed. 'Shelagh, this is Abbey Mitchell.'

'I'm very glad to meet you, Abbey,' said Shelagh, her voice attractively husky, and perfectly even teeth flashing between coral pink lips as she smiled.

She looked as if she belonged, Abbey thought while she murmured something appropriate in return, and a stab of jealousy tore at her insides in a way she had never experienced before.

'I'm afraid we shall have to call off your sitting for this morning, Abbey,' Hammond's deep voice siphoned through her thoughts. 'I have business to attend to, and it will take all day.'

'I understand,' Abbey retorted stiffly, her throat tightening as her mind conjured up its own version of the 'business' which Hammond had referred to and, turning away disconsolately, she murmured, 'I hope you have a pleasant day.'

'I'm sure we shall,' Hammond's amused voice lashed her, but she walked on, not daring to glance back for fear of him noticing the tears brimming her eyes.

'Business!' she snorted furiously, dashing the tears impatiently from her eyes with the back of her hand as she walked away into the veld without really caring which direction she took. What business could a man like Hammond have to attend to which would involve a beautiful woman like Shelagh Varney? He was a wanderer, a penniless artist, but he had obviously acquired a taste for women with class and a dash of wealth thrown in.

A dreadful suspicion crowded her mind. Was that how he made a living? Had he sunk so low that he would make love to a beautiful woman, and accept money from her in return?

Oh, no, *no*! It was too horrible to even think of, and she could not, in all sincerity, imagine Hammond as such a vile sort of person. He was attractive, in a rugged sort of way, and she had no doubt that he was an expert lover. Women would find him irresistible, and would be drawn to him, as she had been, by that vital aura of masculinity he exuded. His magnetism was undeniable, and it was possible, of course, that women like Shelagh Varney pestered him, instead of the opposite. Hammond was a man with a strong sexual appetite; Abbey had sensed this almost from her first encounter with him. Why, then, should he turn his back on what women offered him so readily?

She was driving that painful sword deeper into her own heart with every thought that flashed through her mind, but she was incapable of doing anything about it. She loved him, regardless of what he was, and she could not bear the agonising thought of another woman in his arms.

Abbey returned home eventually, but it was the start of the longest day she had ever lived through. The minutes dragged like hours, and she somehow could not prevent herself from going out to Hammond's camping site that afternoon, but it was an excursion that left her feeling worse than before. His jeep had gone, and so had the Mercedes, and their absence filled her with thoughts and suspicions which tortured her unmercifully.

Hammond did not return to the farm until late on Sunday evening, and it was quite by chance that she heard his jeep roaring across the veld towards his caravan. His return, however, gave her no peace, and she spent a restless night wondering where he had been, and to what extent Shelagh Varney was responsible for his absence from Sweet Waters.

When Abbey awoke on Monday morning she decided against going for her usual sitting to Hammond's caravan. She was too upset, and her mind was in too much of a turmoil to face him, but as the day wore on she came close to regretting her decision. Hammond was on her mind every second of the day, and staying away from him was a punishment in itself, but she was determined not to give in to the urgent plea of her heart.

She went riding at dawn on the Tuesday morning, and Nomad had become so accustomed to the familiar route she took, that he started off at a brisk gallop without much guidance from Abbey. She enjoyed these early morning jaunts across the open veld with Nomad's powerful body beneath her, and the wind whistling past her ears, combing wildly through her shoulder-length hair. She was at peace that morning, with her mind cleared of all its disturbing thoughts, and she would invariably return to the house feeling refreshed and relaxed—but not for long. One glance across the spacious lawns in the general direction of Hammond's caravan would activate her thoughts, and she knew that the rest of the day would be sheer torture.

There were various degrees of torture, she soon discovered. Nomad was taking her home at a slow canter when Hammond stepped directly into their path some metres ahead, and Abbey's heart leapt wildly at the sight of him. His faded denims clung to his lean hips and muscled thighs, and the blue silk sweater clung to his wide shoulders and chest like a second skin. He was a magnificent specimen of masculine virility, and her senses stirred as always at the sight of him, but his tight-lipped expression stilled that flutter of anticipation within her. She was afraid suddenly, and tempted to urge Nomad on past Hammond's imposing figure where he waited up ahead, but her hands tightened automatically on the reins, and the animal slowed down to a walk until they reached Hammond's side.

'Where were you yesterday?' he demanded harshly, his hand gripping Nomad's bridle, and the animal pricked back his ears as if in protest at the tone of his voice.

'Does it matter?' she snapped, resorting to anger as her only defence.

'Naturally it matters.'

'Where were you all weekend?' she counter-questioned sharply.

'I was away on business,' he said, his expression cool and forbidding as he repeated his query. 'Where were you yesterday?'

'I was at home,' she announced, remaining proudly on Nomad's back, and forcing Hammond to look up at her for some silly reason she could not even explain to herself.

'Why didn't you come for your sitting?'

'How was I to know that you were back?' she argued, unable to meet his eyes, but the telltale redness in her cheeks gave her away.

'You know damn well that I waited for you all morning,' he accused harshly, and guilt sent a wave of unreasonable anger rushing through her.

'I have never claimed to possess extra sensory perception,' she informed him sarcastically with a hint of unfamiliar haughtiness in her manner. 'If you needed me for a sitting, then you could have found some way of letting me know.'

'You're behaving like a petulant child, Abbey,' he laughed unexpectedly, and his laughter merely fanned the flame of her fury.

'Remove your hand from the bridle,' she instructed coldly.

'I'll let go when you start behaving yourself.'

Abbey could not explain to herself afterwards what devilish emotion had prompted her actions, but she raised her riding crop and struck him a vicious blow across the left cheek. Horrified, she stared at the angry red weal appearing beneath the skin from his temple down to his chin, and, before she could express her remorse, she was jerked roughly out of the saddle to land in an ungainly heap at his feet. The riding crop was wrenched from her hand and snapped in two across his raised knee, then she was dragged to her feet and, with her arms twisted painfully behind her back, she was crushed against the hard, immovable wall of his chest.

The sparks of green fury in his eyes chilled the blood in her veins, and filled her with a choking fear, then his hard mouth crushed her soft lips against her teeth until the taste of blood was in her mouth. Held helpless in those punishing arms, she could do nothing but endure the pain, and she almost welcomed the wave of darkness which threatened to engulf her.

An eternity seemed to pass before Hammond raised his head, and although she felt weak and drained, her fury had by no means diminished. Throwing back her head in a gesture of defiance, she hissed, 'Let me go, you brute!'

'You will be at my caravan within an hour, or I will come and collect you personally, and I can promise you that I shan't be gentle with you,' he snarled at her.

'You can go to the devil!' she cried, her eyes brimming with angry tears, and her futile efforts to escape his arms merely causing her more pain.

She tried to avoid his descending lips, but while one hand held her arms firmly in place behind her back, the other grasped a handful of her hair, causing fresh tears to fill her eyes when a sharp pain shot through her scalp.

Contrary to what she had expected, his lips were teasing instead of punishing, and her resistance crumbled like a house of cards, leaving her mind devoid of everything except the emotions he was arousing so effortlessly. Shelagh Varney was forgotten in that moment, and nothing mattered beyond the fact that she loved this man.

'For God's sake, Hammond, stop it!' she begged huskily when his lips had tantalised her beyond her endurance.

'Do you apologise for striking me?'

'Yes, yes, I do.'

'Then *say* it, dammit!'

'I apologise for striking you,' she managed unsteadily, delicious little tremors coursing their way along her nervous system when his teeth nipped her ear.

'And you'll never do it again?' he prompted dictatorially.

'I—I'll never do it again,' she promised, and her lips parted eagerly beneath his the next instant.

'That hour has shrunk to forty-five minutes,' he informed her at length, and his expression was stern when she drew his head down to hers so that she could press her lips gently against the angry weal on his cheek.

'Forgive me,' she whispered in a voice husky with remorse, then she escaped from his arms and walked swiftly to where Nomad stood pawing the ground impatiently. 'I shall be at your disposal at the stipulated time.'

She was in the saddle and riding like the wind across the veld before he could reply, and there was a delightful song in her heart which was tempered only by intense regret. She should not have struck him; it had been a totally unforgivable act, and something which she had never imagined herself capable of. She had deserved the punishment he had dished out, and her lips still ached with the memory, just as Hammond must still be feeling the sting of her riding crop.

Abbey lingered only long enough at home to grab a quick slice of toast and a cup of coffee before going out to meet Hammond. Shelagh Varney was temporarily, but not entirely forgotten, and Abbey had been sitting perfectly still on the high stool for almost an hour before Shelagh's beautiful image leapt prominently into her mind.

'She's very beautiful,' Abbey said, breaking the silence between Hammond and herself.

'Who?' he asked absently.

'Shelagh Varney.'

'Yes, she is,' he agreed, twisting the sword in her heart, and she glanced at him warily.

'Have you known her long?'

'Two years.'

'Have there been other women in between?'

'A few,' he smiled cynically, giving that sword a decisive, agonising twist.

'I'm surprised she hasn't objected.'

'Shelagh Varney and I have a perfect understanding,' he assured her with that hateful hint of mockery in his voice, and she stared at him a little incredulously.

'She must be unique,' she could not help remarking sarcastically.

'You don't find women like her very often,' Hammond agreed cynically, and she looked away from him towards the swift running water in the stream to hide the pain in her eyes.

'Are you going to marry her some day?'

'Marriage wouldn't suit Shelagh and me,' Hammond told her tersely. 'The arrangement we have at the moment is near perfect.'

'I see,' Abbey sighed unhappily.

What else was there to say? What *could* she say? The 'near perfect' arrangement between them naturally meant that Shelagh was his mistress, and neither of them seemed to have the inclination to alter the situation.

She had been a fool to fall in love with Hammond. He had not asked for her love, but she had given it all the same, and that left her exactly nowhere. She would join the ranks of the many women who had crossed his path without leaving the slightest impression, and it was this thought which hurt most of all.

'I won't be needing you here tomorrow,' Hammond set the seal on her unhappiness. 'The portrait is done except for the finishing touches.'

'May I see it now?' she asked, sliding tiredly off the stool, but his face assumed that forbidding expression she had encountered once before.

'I said you could see it when it was completed to my satisfaction.'

'And when will that be?'

'I can't say for sure,' he shrugged, wiping his hands on an old cloth and looking strangely preoccupied.

'Well . . .' she sighed, a sudden chill of loneliness gripping her at the realisation that she was being shut out from something she would have wished very much to share. There was always that invisible barrier which he erected whenever she came too close, and she could not help wondering why. 'I'd better go,' she ended lamely.

'You'd better,' he agreed, and she was filled with the aching suspicion that she no longer existed for him.

She wondered what had been the cause of this sudden bout of frowning preoccupation, and she took a wary step towards him. 'Hammond?'

'Hm . . .?'

His eyes met hers, but she had an odd feeling that he was looking through her without actually seeing her and, swallowing down her rising bitterness, she said flatly, 'Nothing.'

She turned away from him, praying that he would call her back, or suggest walking a short distance of the way with her, but he did neither, and her disappointment and unhappiness became a heavy load within her that grew weightier with every step.

Abbey wished that she could understand him, but, more than that, she wished that she could understand *herself*. Twice she had told him that she loved him, but instead of her confession opening the door to some sort of future, she had come up against a blank, impenetrable wall. He had said that he no longer needed her now that the portrait was almost completed, but she could not believe that his interest in her, as a woman, ended there as well, or was she simply deluding herself to the truth which was staring her so blatantly in the face?

'Don't forget Shelagh Varney,' that disturbing little voice reminded her cruelly, and she quickened her pace, her hands clenched at her sides in agitation as she crossed the lawn and ran up the steps into the house.

'I have to go to Pietermaritzburg on business tomorrow morning,' her father announced at the dinner table that evening, and his eyes met Abbey's briefly. 'Would you like to come along to keep me company?'

'I might as well,' she sighed, toying with her food. 'I have nothing else to do.'

'Perhaps you could do a bit of shopping for me while

you're there,' her mother suggested eagerly, and Abbey
nodded listlessly.

She was not very keen to accompany her father on
this trip into Pietermaritzburg, but it would at least be
preferable to moping about the house, or perhaps being
tempted to force her unwanted presence on a man who
had no need of her.

'You're not eating, Abbey,' her mother interrupted
her disturbed thoughts.

'I'm not very hungry.'

'But you've hardly eaten a thing,' Claire protested
and, pushing aside her plate, Abbey rose agitatedly from
the table.

'Don't fuss, Mother.'

Excusing herself, Abbey left the dining-room and
walked out on to the terrace in search of fresh air on
this stifling evening. It was there, in the darkness, that
her father found her some time later, and he draped a
comforting arm about her shoulders.

'Is it Hammond?' he asked with shrewd understanding
when she leaned against him for a moment.

'It's Hammond,' she confessed, adding with false breez-
iness, 'It's nothing, though, that time won't rectify.'

She was not so certain about the latter, however. Time
might convince him of her love for him, but that was no
guarantee that he would eventually feel the same about
her. Shelagh Varney still had to be taken into account, and
his association with her had lasted two years despite the
women in between. 'What chance do I have,' Abbey
wondered, 'of becoming the only woman in his life?'

Armed with her mother's list of requirements, Abbey
walked the busy streets of Pietermaritzburg until, laden
with parcels, she met her father for lunch in a restaurant.
She had not imagined that shopping for her mother

would involve so much walking, and her new sandals were chafing her feet. Her appetite was practically non-existent and, at one stage during the delicious meal, she wondered what she was doing there when every part of her being yearned to be with Hammond.

For some inexplicable reason she was tense and agitated. She wanted to go home, and as quickly as possible, but her father had not completed his business, and it was after three that afternoon before they finally left Pietermaritzburg.

'Do you think I could invite Hammond over for dinner one evening?' she asked her father when they were almost home.

'I don't see why not,' he replied pleasantly.

'I suppose Mother will disapprove strongly,' she sighed unhappily.

'I could always talk her into it.'

'Would you?' Abbey asked seriously, and he smiled and patted her hand gently.

'I'll speak to her this evening, and I'm sure you'll have nothing to worry about.'

Eagle's Peak reared its head beyond the hills, and with an inward sigh of relief Abbey knew that they would soon be home.

Everything looked so blessedly normal when they arrived at the house that she could almost laugh at herself now for being so unnecessarily edgy. She wanted to take a walk down to Hammond's caravan, but her mother had prepared an early dinner, and Abbey was forced to make a pretence of eating while everything within her cried out impatiently to be with Hammond.

'I think you ought to know,' Claire announced while Abbey was hurriedly drinking her coffee, 'Mr Scott has gone.'

'Gone?' Abbey demanded, almost choking on the last

mouthful of hot liquid. 'Gone where?'

'How should I know where he's gone to?' her mother replied coldly, and a chilling sensation was spiralling through Abbey as she put down her cup, and dabbed at her mouth with her table napkin.

'Do you mean he's gone away on business?'

'No,' Claire shook her head. 'He's packed up his caravan, and left for a destination unknown.'

Abbey's insides began to shake, and she exchanged a brief glance with her father before she asked anxiously, 'Did he leave a message for me? A letter, perhaps?'

'I'm afraid he didn't,' her mother replied. 'He merely said he was leaving, and asked me to thank your father for allowing him the privilege of making use of the farm for artistic material, as he put it.'

'Oh, my God!' Abbey whispered, her face as white as chalk, and a searing pain wrenching her insides.

'I can't imagine why you're so upset about it, Abbey,' her mother continued airily. 'He was nothing but a scrounging artist, and he'll never be anything else.'

'I wouldn't have cared if he was a tramp,' Abbey croaked, her eyes blind with misery. 'I happen to love him, Mother.'

There was a startled, incredulous silence, then her mother exclaimed laughingly, 'Don't be ridiculous!'

'It's the truth,' Abbey managed to force the words past her stiff, unwilling lips, and she was surprised somehow to see her mother lose a fraction of her healthy colour.

'Well, he obviously didn't return your feelings,' Claire nailed home the agonising truth.

'Claire!' Edward barked furiously, but Abbey was already on her feet and walking blindly from the room.

Shocked, and utterly shattered, she stumbled into her bedroom and closed the door firmly behind her. She had never dared to hope too much, but, God knows, she had never expected *this*. Had she meant so little to Hammond that he could simply pack up and walk out of her life in this callous way?

No, no, *no*! She wouldn't believe it! She *couldn't*! But he was gone ... without a word ... and what more proof could anyone ask for?

It was as if her world had crashed about her, and the tears spilled from her lashes on to her pale cheeks. She stood there shaking uncontrollably, then a choking sob rose in her throat and she flung herself across her bed. With her face buried in the pillow, she wept unrestrainedly, and great racking sobs tore through her slender body ceaselessly until she lay drained and exhausted. She felt curiously dead inside, and when her father finally walked into her room, closing the door softly behind him, she sat up slowly and looked at him with red-rimmed, lifeless eyes.

'I'm sorry, Abbey,' he said quietly, seating himself beside her on the bed and taking her into his arms. 'I'm sorry, my girl.'

'Oh, Dad,' she sighed tiredly. 'What am I going to do?'

'I wish I had an answer to that,' he said, brushing her hair away from her face with a gentle, comforting hand.

'How could he simply leave without even saying goodbye?'

'You saw him yesterday,' her father remarked probingly. 'Did anything happen, perhaps, to make you suspect that he intended leaving here today?'

She shook her head helplessly. 'He told me that the portrait was almost completed, that he didn't need me to sit for him again, and then——'

'And then?' her father prompted when she paused abruptly.

'He seemed to be a little preoccupied,' she explained. 'I found it strange, and it worried me at first, but I—I eventually presumed that he must have been absorbed in thoughts of a creative nature. There was, after all, the portrait which still needed its finishing touches, and I imagined he was thinking of making a few more sketches for his selection of landscapes.' She tried to think; to concentrate, but her mind refused to function beyond the facts, and she ended up sighing helplessly. 'That was all.'

'I can't understand it,' Edward frowned.

'Neither can I,' she confessed, her lips trembling, 'and I wish—oh, how I wish he'd said something to me instead of leaving the way he did!'

'Perhaps he'll write to you at a later date,' her father consoled her, and she glanced up at him hopefully.

'Do you really think so?'

His arms tightened about her, and he kissed her tenderly on her tear-ravaged cheek before he released her. 'I hope, for your sake, that he does.'

Her father had lit a little flame of hope inside of her, but it petered out the moment she was alone. Hammond had never given her reason to hope for more, and his interest in her could only have been less than casual, if the manner in which he had departed from the farm was anything to judge by.

A fresh bout of tears overtook her, and she cried herself into an exhausted sleep that night from which she mercifully did not awaken until dawn the following morning.

Abbey went for a long ride that morning, taxing Nomad's strength to the utmost as they flew across the earth at a wild pace. The smell of horseflesh and leather and fresh, dewy grass was all around her, but instead of the peace and tranquillity she always acquired from this exercise, there was only that dreadful gnawing pain of knowing that she had lost something vital.

Without actually intending to do so, she found herself riding towards the stream where Hammond's caravan had been parked. There was nothing there, of course, except the usual traces that someone had camped there, and clear tyre marks in the sand indicated his departure. Her throat tightened with tears, and she pulled agitatedly at the reins. Nomad turned round obediently, and his thundering hooves echoed across the veld until they reached the waterfall.

'What am I doing here?' she asked herself, but she knew the agonising truth. There were memories bound up in this enchanted place which she would remember until the day she died; memories of an awakening love, and of a brief, shared passion. If Hammond had felt nothing else for her, then he had at least desired her, but this thought offered her little comfort as she slid off Nomad's back and tethered him to a tree.

With the sound of cascading water in her ears, she knelt beside the pool and trailed her fingers in the shimmering water. They had bathed in its crystal clear depths, touching, kissing, and loving. No, that was not quite the truth. *She* had loved, while *he* had merely indulged in an experiment to see how far he could make her go.

Squirming inwardly, she scooped water into her hands and drank it thirstily, but the taste of defeat was in her mouth, and the water was bitter-sweet.

She wiped her lips with the back of her hand, and a few moments later she leapt on to Nomad's back, urging him into a wild gallop, and the animal obeyed her with a tireless energy.

Abbey drove into Bergville after breakfast that morning, and went straight to the hotel. Her brief enquiry at the reception desk left her with as little information as before, except that Hammond had left instructions that his post was to be returned to whatever address was on the back of the envelope.

He would write to her, of course he would, she tried to tell herself when she arrived back at the farm, but, as the days passed and lengthened into a week, she gradually began to lose hope.

Abbey waited two weeks before she was able to convince herself that Hammond had no intention of contacting her in any way, and it was on a bleak Monday morning that she packed her suitcases and informed her parents that she was returning to Durban. She could not stay at Sweet Waters. Not *now*! Not with all those painful memories eating away at her insides. Her father understood even though he begged her to stay, but her mother had remained strangely silent and, as she drove away from her home, Abbey knew that the incredible loneliness she had once visualised had now become a reality. The future lay before her like an empty, yawning chasm, and the only man who could fill it had placed himself totally beyond her reach.

Why, why, why? the question reverberated through her tortured mind. Why did he have to leave like that? Why hadn't he said something? Why didn't he write! And *why* had fate decreed that she should love a man who could never care for her in return?

'Oh, God!' she groaned and, pulling the Porsche off the road, she switched off the engine and buried her ashen face in her trembling hands.

Tears of desolation and despair trickled through her fingers, and it was a long while before she was capable of continuing her journey with a certain amount of calmness and control. Durban was still a long way ahead of her, and she somehow had to get on with the job of living.

CHAPTER EIGHT

ABBEY had always prided herself on being a sensible, realistic person, and although she had slipped somewhat in this respect, she soon pulled herself together and telephoned her previous employers. They were kind enough to offer her a temporary post with the possibility of something more permanent as soon as a vacancy arose, and that was good enough for her.

She had to work; she had to keep herself physically and mentally occupied, and for this reason she did anything and everything that came her way, often putting in long hours at the office to arrive home at night too exhausted to think, and often too tired to eat. Despair and longing became a part of her daily existence, and she could never quite put out that tiny flame of hope that Hammond might yet contact her, but after three weeks in Durban her hopes turned to cold ashes.

When her doorbell rang unexpectedly one Saturday afternoon her thoughts leapt at once to Hammond, and this resulted in her staring a little foolishly at Jeanette Halstead, whose regal presence graced her doorstep.

'May I come in, Abbey?'

Abbey came to her senses abruptly, and opened the door wider with a hand that shook slightly. 'Yes, of course, Mrs Halstead.'

The older woman glanced about her with obvious curiosity as she stepped inside and, when they were seated in Abbey's lounge, she said with unusual warmth, 'This is the first time I've had the opportunity of seeing your flat, and I must say that you have furnished it with extreme taste, my dear.'

'Thank you,' Abbey replied, startled by the compliment, and more than a little wary of it.

'You're wondering why I'm here, no doubt,' Jeanette Halstead remarked, placing her bandbag on the floor beside her chair, and clasping her hands elegantly in her lap.

'I presume it has something to do with Derek.'

Jeanette smiled, but her dark eyes remained cool and watchful. 'You're very astute, but then Derek always said you were.'

'Is he ill?' Abbey asked a little anxiously, but the woman seated opposite her shook her head.

'Not ill, my dear. Just very unhappy.'

Abbey lowered her eyes, hiding her discomfort. 'I'm sorry.'

'Will you see him if he calls on you?'

Abbey's lips tightened. 'Derek should know me better than to imagine I'd slam the door in his face, but——'

'Derek doesn't know yet that you've returned to Durban,' Jeanette told her hastily, 'and I confess that I'm here without his knowledge.'

Abbey stared at her contemplatively for a moment, then she asked: 'How did you know I was back, Mrs Halstead?'

'Your mother telephoned me, of course,' she confirmed Abbey's suspicions. 'Why?'

'I merely wondered,' Abbey sighed with a touch of bitterness, 'but I should have known she would do something like that sooner or later.'

Jeanette eyed her curiously. 'You seem annoyed.'

'I'm not annoyed, Mrs Halstead,' Abbey explained. 'I'm merely tired of having my life manipulated.'

There was an awkward little silence during which

Abbey realised that Jeanette Halstead, like her mother, would never understand her feelings in this matter.

'May I tell Derek that you're back, and that you'll see him?' Jeanette asked at length, wearing her sweetest and most persuasive expression.

'I'll see Derek, Mrs Halstead,' Abbey agreed, choosing her words carefully. 'But please don't imagine that I'll consider becoming engaged to him again, and don't, whatever you do, give him that impression.'

When Jeanette Halstead had gone, leaving behind only a lingering trace of her expensive perfume, Abbey wondered whether agreeing to see Derek had not been a mistake. Would his mother make it clear to him that he should not expect too much, and would he, in himself, be satisfied with a friendship which would have no strings attached to it? Abbey was suddenly not so sure, and with a sigh of irritation which was tinged with despair, she went through to the bathroom to wash her hair, and rinse out a few of her lacy undergarments.

She hated weekends. She invariably found herself with nothing to do during those long hours before she could return to the office on the Monday morning. All she could think of was Hammond, and every thought intensified the longing until she wanted to scream. Where was he? What was he doing? Was he with Shelagh Varney, or was he seeking a diversion with someone else in much the same way he did with her? Abbey groaned inwardly as these agonising thoughts ricocheted through her mind, torturing her to the point of madness. If she could remember Shelagh Varney's post-office box number, then she could write to Hammond, she supposed, but she still had some pride left. If she had meant anything to him at all, then he would not have left Sweet Waters without saying goodbye. He had promised her that she would see her portrait as soon as he had completed it, but that promise, along with everything else, had obviously meant nothing at all.

'Oh, lord!' she groaned and, pulling herself together with an effort, she dried her hair and tied it back from her face before seeing to her clothes.

Abbey had not expected to see Derek quite so soon after his mother's visit that afternoon, and she was more than a little startled when she opened the door that evening to find him standing there so tall and lean, and with a boyishly uncertain smile on his handsome face. There was a time when that smile would have warmed her heart with what she had imagined was love. That warmth was somehow still there, but she recognised it now as fondness, and nothing more.

'Come in, Derek,' she invited quietly, and, closing the door behind him, she led the way into the lounge.

'I couldn't believe my ears when Mother told me this evening that you'd returned,' Derek told her when he had seated himself in the chair which he had always favoured most.

'I never planned to stay away for ever,' she replied, her eyes on his fair hair which shone like spun gold in the light of the lamp.

'You resigned your job.'

'I resigned because I had no idea at the time how long I'd be away. I needed to go home, and I needed time to get things into perspective.'

'And did you?'

His eyes were intent upon her face, and she looked away hastily. 'I would say that I discovered a great deal about myself which I hadn't known before, but I don't wish to discuss it.'

There was an awkward silence before he asked, 'Have you made any decisions about your future?'

'I'll take each day as it comes.'

'And what about us, Abbey?'

This was the question she had feared most, but perhaps it was best that they dealt with it, and got it over with quickly, she decided as she met his glance unwaveringly. 'Don't ask me to resume our engagement, Derek, because I can't.'

'What about friendship?' he persisted, and Abbey nodded at once.

'I would like that, but not if you're still hoping it might lead to something more serious.'

Derek frowned long and hard at the patterned carpet beneath his expensive shoes, then he raised his glance and said with familiar determination, 'I'll never stop hoping, Abbey, but you have my word that I shan't pressurise you into anything that you don't want.'

'Haven't I hurt you enough?' she asked with some amazement, and he smiled at her a little sadly.

'I'd be hurt more if you shut me out of your life completely,' he announced, and there was nothing she could reply to that.

She observed him closely for a moment, but, instead of seeing Derek, she saw Hammond's tall, broad-shouldered frame. She would have given anything at that moment to have Hammond sitting there in one of her chairs as she so often had seen him sprawl in those faded canvas chairs used for camping. He would light a cigarette and watch the smoke curl lazily into the air, or he would smile at her in that mocking, faintly sensuous way which never failed to quicken her pulse rate in that extraordinary manner.

Abbey pressed her fingers against her eyelids in a desperate attempt to shut out the image her mind had conjured up before her. When she opened them again it was Derek she saw in the chair opposite her own, but there was nothing she could do about the pain that tore through her insides like a searing flame licking against an open wound.

'I'll put the kettle on and make us a cup of coffee,' she said, getting to her feet rather abruptly.

'That's an excellent idea.'

When Derek left that evening she bathed and went to bed, but she couldn't sleep. She had lost count of the many times she had gone over and over every little incident in her mind, searching for a possible clue to Hammond's abrupt departure from Sweet Waters, and finding herself left with only the despairing knowledge that she never did and never could mean anything to him. It was an unpalatable thought; loving him so much and knowing that he did not care for her in return, and if this agony was what loving was all about, then she could have done without it very nicely.

Flinging back the covers, she slipped out of bed and switched on the light. A glass of warm milk might help her to sleep, she decided, but when she passed the dressing table mirror she paused abruptly. The face that stared back at her was almost the face of a stranger. Pale and gaunt, with shadows which had become a permanent fixture beneath lifeless eyes, she was nothing like her former self. Self-pity was something which she knew she had to avoid at all costs if she were to survive, but it reigned supreme in that moment, and she burst into tears.

'Oh, Hammond, Hammond, what have you done to me?' she wept pitifully into her hands, and it was a long time before she was able to control herself sufficiently to go through to the bathroom. It was senseless to cry like this, she told herself firmly as she splashed cold water into her face. It only made her feel and look worse. She would not cry again; not for Hammond, and she raised her chin and squared her shoulders as she switched off the bathroom light and went into the kitchen.

Abbey pampered herself a little when she finally returned to her bedroom and, propped up against the pillows, she drank her glass of warm milk slowly and made a firm resolution not to think of Hammond again.

Exiling him from her mind was easier said than done, she discovered during the weeks that followed. During idle moments he leapt into her thoughts like a demon intent upon causing her pain, and it was always with the greatest difficulty that she would succeed in evicting him once more. Derek's company helped a great deal to ward off the loneliness during the weekends, and he occasionally took her out to dinner during the week. His friendship was as undemanding as he had promised, and because of this Abbey had finally allowed herself to relax in his company.

It came as a surprise, and a certain amount of shock, when Dalene burst into her flat one evening like a raging spitfire intent upon doing damage.

'I want to talk to you,' she snapped, rudely skipping the preliminaries of politeness. 'You're not going to mess up Derek's life as you did once before.'

'I have——'

'You dangled him on a string for eighteen months before you finally agreed to marry him, and you were engaged only two weeks when you broke it off,' Dalene continued as if Abbey had not spoken. 'The scandal still causes a stir among our friends, and I won't let you do this to him again.'

'Dalene, I——'

'I warned Derek all along, but he wouldn't listen. I told him that you're not the wife for him, and I was proved right,' Dalene interrupted her rudely once more, her dark eyes spitting pure venom. 'You're hardly back in the city and you already have him running after you like a lovesick fool, and I'm damned if I'm going to let you hurt him again. You're to leave him alone, do you hear!'

Dalene had been shouting so loudly that Abbey's ears had vibrated uncomfortably, but when Dalene paused for breath, Abbey seized the opportunity with her usual determination, and said sharply, 'Will you shut up for a minute and allow me to speak?'

'I'm listening,' Dalene announced, her hands on her hips and her eyes challenging, 'but whatever it is you have to say, it had better be good.'

Abbey's annoyance became a red-hot anger, but she suppressed it forcibly, and said with surprising calmness, 'I have no intention of marrying Derek. Not now . . . not ever . . . and Derek knows that. We have agreed to be friends, and nothing more.'

'Friends?' Dalene snorted cynically. 'Don't be a fool, Abbey. Derek is still hoping he'll be able to make you change your mind, and don't tell me you're not aware of that.'

'I'm aware of it, but he sees me of his own free will, and I have no intention of slamming the door in his face when next he comes here,' Abbey answered stubbornly. 'I respect him too much to do that.'

Abbey had been speaking literally as well as figuratively, but Dalene laughed shrewishly, pushing Abbey's blood pressure up several degrees in the process. 'You may respect him,' Dalene accused, 'but you don't give a damn how much you hurt him.'

'Dalene, I suggest you have a chat with your mother,' Abbey sighed exasperatedly. 'She came here a few weeks ago and practically paved the way to my door on Derek's behalf. She asked if I would allow him to visit me, and I raised no objections. I might not want to marry Derek, but I certainly won't treat him like a leper. He knows and understands my feelings, just as I know and respect his, and I certainly have no intention of brushing aside his friendship.

There was a tense, angry silence as they faced each other sparringly in Abbey's dimly lit lounge, then Dalene hissed accusingly, 'You just don't care, do you?'

Abbey was becoming infinitely tired of this conversation, but she nevertheless managed to control her temper. 'I care very much, Dalene,' she assured the younger girl, 'and I'd agree right this minute not to see him again, but I know that if I did it would hurt him much more.'

'You think you have all the answers, don't you?' Dalene retorted, flinging out her arms in an angry gesture, and this time Abbey's endurance reached its limit.

'I think you've overstayed your welcome,' she told Dalene in an icy voice which she barely recognised as her own. 'You've tried my patience to the limit, and if you don't leave now I'll have you thrown out!'

Dalene went white, then she hissed threateningly, 'You haven't seen the last of me yet!'

'If you come here again, Dalene, I'll have you arrested as an intruder, and that *would* look nice in the Sunday papers,' Abbey warned. 'I'm sure your parents would be thrilled at the publicity their daughter would get.'

Dalene went whiter still, and her face became distorted with rage. 'Why, you——'

'Go home, Dalene,' Abbey interrupted, walking away from her to open the door. 'Go home, and grow up.'

For one brief moment Abbey thought that Dalene was preparing herself for a physical attack. She was clenching and unclenching her hands at her sides, but she controlled herself visibly, and stormed out of

Abbey's flat in much the same manner she had arrived earlier.

Abbey was shaking inwardly when she closed the door, and locked it. It had been a distressing encounter which she hoped would not be repeated at some future date, and although she had no real intention of carrying out her threats, she felt it necessary to discuss Dalene's visit with Derek when next she met him.

'I'll have a word with Dalene,' Derek promised a few evenings later when she had told him of his sister's visit, and what had transpired between them. 'She owes you an apology, and I'll see to it that she doesn't trouble you again.'

'Please, Derek,' she begged hastily, 'don't make too much of the incident. In a way, I suppose, she had your interests at heart, and I merely thought you ought to know. Perhaps, if you talked to her, a repetition might be avoided.'

'It was quite right of you to tell me,' Derek frowned at her, 'and I shall certainly have a very serious chat to her.'

Abbey had expected it to end there, but a few days later she received a note of apology from Dalene. It was, she suspected, written under duress, but she accepted it at face value, and decided to put the incident in the past where it belonged.

Three months had passed since Abbey's return to Durban, and during this time Christmas had come and gone with spectacular uneventfulness. The new year was now well into its second month, but Abbey did not want to think of the empty future ahead of her. She had spoken to her father on the telephone a few times, and once only to her mother, but she had not gone home again for a weekend. She could not return as yet to the

place where she had found and lost her love so swiftly.
Sweet Waters was her home, but too many painful
memories lurked there, and the pain was something she
was only beginning to learn to live with. She had tried
her hand at sketching again to fill the empty hours, but
she had relinquished the idea when Hammond's face
had appeared on every sketch she had made. She could
not forget him, it was an impossible task, and she knew
in her heart that she never would. He had become a
part of her which she would never be without, and even
if she never saw him again, she would carry his image
locked away in her memory for the rest of her life.

She was happy in her job, even though she had not,
as yet, been offered a permanent post, but she was quite
happy to continue as she was, helping out in all the
departments of the architectural firm, and gaining
knowledge as she went along. They had been more than
kind to her, and she did not stint herself in her services.

She owed a great deal to Derek. Unlike their earlier
relationship, he now considered her more, and never
once did he try to overpower her with his feelings. If he
still loved her, then he kept it to himself, and never once
did he force his company on her unless she wished it.
Abbey preferred it that way, but her life had become an
empty shell; a daily existence of going to the office, and
returning home in the evenings to an empty, silent flat.
The occasional dinner appointment with Derek was
therefore a welcome change from the monotony.

'What happened, Abbey?' Derek asked on one such
evening when he had taken her out for a meal to a quiet
restaurant, and his troubled glance was intent upon her
thin, grave face. 'You're not the bright, smiling girl I
used to know, and you've lost a great deal of weight
these past months.'

Abbey sipped at her strong, aromatic coffee and

gestured vaguely with a slender hand. 'Perhaps I'm working too hard in the hope of a permanent job at the office.'

Surprise lifted his eyebrows a fraction higher. 'Is that so important to you?'

'It's important that I keep myself busy, and whether I like it or not, I must think of the future.'

'You're not happy, and I've known that for a long time,' he observed, his glance probing hers as he leaned his elbows on the table. 'You wouldn't perhaps like to share your burden with me?'

Abbey stiffened automatically, rejecting instantly his suggestion that she should speak of the one thing she would have given anything to wipe from her memory, but she relaxed gradually when she realised that his suggestion had been motivated by concern.

'I appreciate your kindness, Derek,' she said at length, 'but I can't share my problems with you.'

'Can't, or won't?' he proved relentlessly.

'Very well, then,' she sighed. 'I *won't* share my problems with you, or with anyone else for that matter.'

'Abbey . . .' His hand found hers across the table, but her fingers remained cold and unresponsive beneath his. 'You know I love you, don't you?'

This was the first time in three months that he had broached the subject, and the look in his eyes filled her with such dismay that she lowered her glance. 'Yes, I know.'

'And you know I promised not to pressurise you into anything that you didn't want.'

'Derek, I——'

'Listen to me for a moment,' he interrupted her hastily, his fingers tightening about hers. 'I'm asking you once again to marry me, Abbey, but on this occasion I don't expect an answer from you today, tomorrow, or the day after that. All I'm asking is that you give it some thought, and I'll be satisfied with whatever you eventually decide.'

Abbey stared at him, searching for the right words, but there was no gentle way of rejecting his proposal, and she finally heard herself saying the words she had hoped to avoid. 'I don't love you, Derek.'

'I accept that,' he replied with astonishing amiability, 'but I'm nevertheless asking you to give my proposal a great deal of thought.'

'But——'

'We could be happy together, I know it,' he persisted eagerly. 'Will you consider it, Abbey?'

So many conflicting thoughts rushed through her mind at that moment that she could merely sit and stare at him, but, as her mind emptied, only one thought remained. Derek loved her, she did not doubt that, and, with no hope of Hammond ever caring for her, she might as well consider seeking whatever happiness she could with someone else. Where she had once been confident of living independently without the burden of marital ties, she was now afraid of finally having to face the future alone. It was a devastating thought. Derek would not always be there; he would, in time, tire of waiting, and he would seek his happiness elsewhere. When that happened she would be entirely alone.

'I can't promise you anything,' she said at last in a voice that sounded hollow and lifeless to her own ears, 'but I'll consider it.'

'That's good enough for me,' Derek smiled and, releasing her hand, he ordered a bottle of champagne to be brought to their table.

It was only when she was alone in her flat, later that evening, that Abbey wondered whether she was being fair to Derek. Was it fair to let him go on hoping, and would it be fair to marry him without loving him? She could well imagine Dalene's reply to this, but Derek was fully aware of her feelings, and if he was prepared to marry her under those circumstances, then why should she worry? There was a part of her, however, that disagreed strongly. It was a consoling thought, she decided at length, that Derek would not be rushing her into giving him an answer, for she would have to give the matter careful thought before she confronted him with her decision.

Abbey slept very badly that night, but that was no longer something unusual. She had become accustomed to lying awake nights, listening to the muted sounds of a city which never seemed to sleep. The traffic became less, but it never quite ceased during the night, and she felt a sort of restless affinity with those people down there in the streets, wondering where they were going, where they had come from, and what they were seeking. On this occasion, however, she was wondering more about herself. What was *she* seeking, and what, exactly, did she want from life? The latter was a foolish question, she decided. What she wanted from life was the impossible, and she did not want to dwell on that subject, but that left her with the first part of her question unanswered. *What was she seeking?* She had not sought love, but she had found it, and she could not help thinking that she would have been far more contented had it continued to elude her. Peace of mind was all she sought now, and if a dash of happiness happened to be thrown in for good measure, then she would have nothing to complain about.

It was with this thought in mind that she finally went to sleep, but she was up again long before dawn. She spent the next few nights in a similar manner, her thoughts in a turmoil of indecision, but when Derek paid her a surprise visit on the Sunday morning, she had almost decided to accept his proposal despite that little inner voice which so rigorously rejected the idea.

'I hope you don't mind,' Derek smiled at her a little sheepishly, indicating the newspapers under his arm. 'If you're busy I'll simply sit here quietly and read.'

'I'll put the kettle on and make us a pot of tea,' Abbey said and, leaving him in the lounge, she went through to her small kitchen.

She had contemplated going for a long drive, and perhaps having lunch at one of the coastal resorts further south. Anything would have been preferable to sitting alone in her flat, staring at the buildings across the street, and with nothing but her thoughts for company. Derek's arrival was, in a way, a welcome diversion, and she sighed with a measure of relief as she switched on the kettle and set out the cups.

When she returned to the lounge, some minutes later, she found Derek comfortably seated on the sofa with the newspapers spread out around him. He drank his tea, nibbled at the biscuits she had baked during one of her restless evenings, and they finally discussed at great length the potentiality of the horse everyone predicted would win the July Handicap that year. They did at least have a love of horses in common, she thought at length with a wry smile. The only difference was that Derek loved gambling on horses, while she simply enjoyed riding them.

Derek eventually returned his attention to the newspaper on his lap and, with nothing to do, Abbey picked up a section of the newspaper which he had discarded. They read in silence for a while, but she looked up sharply when Derek rustled his paper with obvious agitation.

'Listen to this,' he said abruptly, folding back the

pages, and flattening with his hand the section he wanted to read. 'Hammond Scott, a newcomer to the world of art, will be exhibiting his paintings in the banqueting hall of the Rembrandt Hotel in Johannesburg, and at a sneak preview critics acclaimed his work as——'

'Let me see that,' Abbey interrupted in a brittle voice, flinging aside the section she had been reading, and almost snatching the newspaper from his hands. With her heart beating heavily against her ribs, she read the rest of the review like someone who had been given a glimpse of food after having been starved almost a lifetime. Her hands were shaking so much that she had to read the item over several times until, with every word branded on her mind, she got to her feet unsteadily, and dropped the paper in Derek's lap. 'The opening night of the exhibition is this coming Friday,' she told him, staring blindly out of the window, and oblivious of the fact that her hands were clenching the windowsill so tightly that her knuckles showed white through the skin.

'You're not thinking of going, are you?' Derek demanded at once, and she heard him thrust aside the paper before he joined her at the window.

'I . . . don't know,' she replied hesitantly but truthfully as she resolutely avoided Derek's probing glance.

'Abbey,' he said at length, breaking the tense silence between them, and turning her about to face him. 'It's Hammond Scott, isn't it? He's been the cause of your unhappiness these past months.' She could not reply, but her pale, pinched expression gave him the answer as clearly as if she had spoken, and he released her abruptly. 'I should have known,' he said almost as though he were speaking to himself, and she knew a sudden desire to explain.

'Whatever there was between Hammond and myself,

I can assure you it was purely one-sided,' she said, opening up those wounds which she knew would never heal entirely, and she had great difficulty in controlling the tremor in her voice as she added huskily, 'I meant nothing to him.'

'Poor Abbey,' Derek sighed, his expression grave as he tucked a strand of dark, silky hair behind her ear and framed her face with his hands. 'We're quite a pair, aren't we?'

'It almost looks as though we belong together,' she smiled shakily.

'It does, doesn't it?' he agreed solemnly, then, for the first time in months, he brushed his lips lightly against hers.

He went out quietly a few minutes later, leaving her alone with her disturbed thoughts, and that renewed bout of pain and longing which lashed her so mercilessly. Derek had left his newspapers behind, and Abbey read the article once more, but the words swam before her eyes, and her hot tears made damp blotches on the paper before she flung it aside, and wept. Curled up in her chair, and with her head resting on her arms, she cried until she felt quite exhausted, but still the tears came. She sat up eventually, and leaned back in her chair with her eyes closed. There were no more sobs racking her body, but the tears continued to flow from beneath her lashes, and they paved their way relentlessly down her pale cheeks. She wiped them away with the tips of her fingers, but others swiftly took their place, and she finally relinquished the effort to control them.

She sat there for a long time, how long she was not quite sure, but her tears had finally dried on her cheeks, and her limbs felt heavy with a fatigue that came from deep within her. She had to think, but her mind refused to function. It had centred itself on one thing only, and, like a faulty record, it repeated one word with agonising persistence. 'Hammond, Hammond, Hammond!'

Those grey-green eyes mocked her, that often sensuous mouth smiled with sardonic amusement, and she was tortured beyond endurance by the memories of those moments they had shared. She had to fight against these reminders of her folly, but at that moment she did not have the strength to do so, and they filtered through her mind slowly and painfully, tearing away at her insides until she wanted to scream with the agony of it.

'Hammond . . . oh, Hammond,' his name spilled from her lips almost like a prayer, or a plea for mercy, but there was no mercy in a mind that would not be stilled. It clawed at the wounds which had been so slow to heal, and the pain started afresh, searing her heart and her soul until she felt certain she would go mad.

She pressed her fingers against her throbbing temples in an effort to think clearly. The opening of Hammond's exhibition was five days away, and she was being torn apart by conflicting thoughts. She desperately wanted to be there on the opening night. She *had* to see him, even if it were only from a distance, but there was another part of her that was terribly afraid of what it might do to her to be so near to him . . . and yet so far. How much pain, she wondered, could she still endure?

CHAPTER NINE

DEREK drove Abbey out to the airport on the Friday afternoon. She had not wanted him to, but he had insisted, and she had been too tired to argue. It had taken a tremendous amount of soul-searching to come to this decision to attend the opening of Hammond's exhibition. There had been so many things against it, but in the end her heart had dictated her actions. She had to see Hammond once more, and she had convinced herself that she would be satisfied even if she did not have the opportunity to speak to him.

'I must confess that I'm not very happy about your going to that exhibition in Johannesburg,' Derek voiced his feelings once again while they waited around in the departure hall for her flight to be called.

'I'll be back again on Sunday,' she tried to reassure him, but he eyed her a little dubiously.

'Will you?'

Anxiety was suddenly mirrored in every line of his handsome face, and she touched his arm lightly. 'Don't look like that, Derek.'

'You will remember that I love you?' he asked, his hand covering hers at once, and clasping it firmly.

'I shall never forget, and . . .' A lump rose in her throat, but she swallowed it down hastily before she said: 'I think I shall be able to give you an answer as soon as I've returned.'

'Abbey . . .' he began, then he paused, seemingly at a loss for words and, drawing her against him, he kissed her on the lips at the very moment her flight was announced.

'I must go,' she whispered hastily, disengaging herself from his arms. 'See you on Sunday.'

At the departure gate she turned and waved once more, then she walked on with the rest of the passengers towards the waiting Boeing.

The flight to Johannesburg lasted an hour, but every minute was an agony of renewed indecision. She had made up her mind, once and for all, to attend Hammond's exhibition, but what if her decision ended in disaster? What would she do if he deliberately snubbed her, and how would she feel if she discovered that Shelagh Varney was still very much in the picture?

'Oh, *damn, damn*!' she cursed herself silently. She could always stay away from the exhibition, she supposed. Nothing and no one was forcing her to attend, and there was still plenty of time to change her mind.

When the Boeing landed at Jan Smuts Airport, Abbey found herself doing things almost automatically. She took the bus into the city, and a taxi took her from the airways terminal to the Morningside Hotel. Her room was situated on the third floor overlooking the busy city street, and she tried not to think of what lay ahead of her as she unpacked her suitcase. She had made her plans, and she would abide by them regardless of what happened.

The telephone directory lay on the table beside the telephone, and she picked it up idly, paging through it until she found what she was looking for. There were plenty of Scotts in Johannesburg, and a few had the initial 'H' tagged on to another, but she could not be sure whether any of them were Hammond, or if, in fact, he even possessed such a thing as a telephone wherever he lived.

She dropped the telephone directory on to the table and went through to the bathroom to run her bath water. She had less than two hours to prepare herself, and she desperately needed a soak in a hot, scented bath to ease the tension from her body, if not from her mind. The opening night of an art exhibition was undoubtedly always a posh affair, and she had decided on her blue silk evening gown with its matching wrap.

Later, when she viewed herself critically in the full-length mirror, she felt reasonably satisfied with the image she projected. Her dark hair had lost none of its lustre, and she had piled it on to her head in a neat yet fashionable style. She had taken a great deal of care with her make-up in an effort to project a cool, calm and sophisticated image, and she hoped fervently that her appearance would see her through this difficult evening that lay before her.

The Rembrandt Hotel was a little more than a block away from the Morningside, and Abbey walked the distance within a few minutes, but she was rigid with nerves when she stepped into the spacious foyer of the banqueting hall where a cocktail party was in progress as a prelude to the opening of the exhibition. The men were all in evening dress, while the women at their sides were fashionably dressed for the occasion, but Abbey paid little attention to them as her nervous glance darted from one end of the crowded foyer to the other without encountering Hammond's familiar figure. Two familiar faces did, however, eventually succeed in catching her eye.

'Dad! Mother!' she exclaimed in surprise, and with a certain amount of relief as she hurried across to where they were standing. 'I never expected to see you here this evening,' she said, kissing them quickly on the cheek.

'Neither did we expect to see you,' Claire announced, looking decidedly agitated, but Abbey was much too nervous to let it trouble her at that precise moment.

'When I read the article in the newspaper—about the exhibition, I—I had to come,' she explained haltingly, conscious of cameras flashing as members of the press took photographs of the celebrities present. 'I flew up this afternoon, and I'm staying at the Morningside Hotel.'

'We thought it best not to let you know, but we

received an invitation from Hammond to attend. I'm hoping to buy the painting he did of our home, and perhaps also a few others,' Edward told her, then his blue gaze wandered over her with critical concern. 'You've lost weight, my girl.'

'I've been working hard,' she shrugged away his observation, then she changed the subject hastily. 'You're staying here at the Rembrandt, I suppose?'

'Hammond very kindly reserved a suite for us, or we might have found it fully booked,' her father replied, and Abbey could barely conceal her surprise, but, before she could say anything, a waiter appeared with a tray of champagne, and they helped themselves to a glass.

Her father was saying something about Nomad missing her, but Abbey barely heard him as her restless glance searched every new arrival until she could not restrain herself from saying anxiously, 'I don't see Hammond anywhere.'

'He hasn't arrived yet,' Claire answered before her husband could, then her eyes met Abbey's accusingly. 'I would have thought that Derek would have the good sense to come with you.'

'No, Mother,' Abbey shook her head. 'I decided to come alone.'

Edward changed the subject, steering their conversation on to safer ground while they drank their champagne, but a stir among the guests finally made them turn to face the entrance of the foyer.

Abbey could never explain afterwards exactly what she felt in that moment when her hungry eyes fastened themselves on to Hammond's tall, broad-shouldered frame, but she did remember going hot, then cold, and her insides shook uncontrollably. He looked so achingly familiar, and yet there was something about him which she found terrifyingly strange. His hair of burnished copper looked deceptively dark in the artificial lighting, and intead of lying across his broad forehead in an unruly fashion, it was clipped short and brushed back severely. The impeccably tailored evening suit increased that feeling of strangeness she was experiencing, but her heart recognised him with a wild, unmanageable thudding which seemed to rise into her throat to choke off her breath.

Hammond was not alone. Shelagh Varney was at his side, her arm linked through his in a possessive manner, and her smile radiant as the cameras flashed repeatedly. Her blonde hair had been done in a stylish yet casual fashion, and her shimmering black evening gown enhanced that look of elegance and sophistication which Abbey had noticed once before. Hammond glanced down at his beautiful companion, and they smiled at each other with an intimacy which stabbed viciously at Abbey's heart.

'That's Shelagh Varney,' she heard her mother whisper to her father. 'She's the woman who came to see him at the farm.'

Hammond stopped to talk to several people, and Shelagh left his side to mingle with a few of the other guests, but Abbey lost sight of her swiftly. She could not take her eyes off Hammond. His rugged features were tanned, but decidedly thinner than she remembered, and as her hungry glance swept him from head to foot, she could not help wondering with a certain amount of compassion whether he had hired his suit. He was receiving plenty of attention with everyone clamouring to speak to him, but, instead of shying away from his important guests, he looked every bit as comfortable in their presence as they did in his. This, Abbey tried to tell herself, was the struggling artist who had come to her engagement party so many months ago dressed in a denim jacket and pants, but she could not quite associate the man she saw with the man she had known. He had never lacked determination and confidence, but she had never seen him so completely in command of a situation, as if mingling with these important people was an everyday occurrence, and it simply intensified the feeling that she was looking at a stranger.

Hammond turned suddenly, and it felt to her as if her heart had stopped beating when those grey-green eyes met hers across the foyer, but her heartbeats rushed on again at an incredible, thundering pace that made her feel quite dizzy as she stared back hypnotically into those compelling eyes. His features were granite-hard, and totally inscrutable, but Abbey went hot and cold in rapid succession, and her hands were shaking so much that she had to put down her glass for fear of dropping it. She saw him say something to the man beside him, and then he was crossing the foyer to where she stood rigidly beside her parents.

'Mr Mitchell,' he smiled faintly in recognition, ignoring Abbey as he shook hands with her father. 'I'm glad you could come,' he said, but his smile faded, and his glance was cool as he inclined his head briefly in her mother's direction. 'Good evening, Mrs Mitchell.'

That deep, familiar voice quivered along Abbey's nerves, and her mouth felt horribly dry when he finally turned to face her. She felt as though she had become suspended in a vacuum as she withstood his piercing glance for interminable seconds, then she held out her hand and said with deceptive calmness, 'Good evening, Hammond.'

For one chilling second she nursed the alarming suspicion that he was going to ignore her, then his large hand enveloped hers, and his touch sent an electrifying

current surging from her fingertips up the length of her
arm to set her nerve-ends quivering madly.

'I hoped you would come, Abbey,' he said, behaving
as if they had parted company only the day before. 'I
have something to show you.'

Without releasing her hand, he pulled her arm
through his, and asked her parents to excuse them.
Abbey was allowed only a brief glimpse of their astonished faces, and then she was being escorted swiftly
through the jostling crowd towards the large doors
leading into the banqueting hall.

Alone with him in that vast hall with somewhere between fifty and sixty paintings either adorning the walls,
or erected on stands, she felt incredibly nervous and not at
all sure what was expected of her. Was Hammond honour-
ing her by allowing her a preview of his work, or did he
want to see her privately for some obscure reason?

Abbey withdrew her arm from his and, placing a
comfortable distance between them, she wandered
among the paintings exhibited, silently admiring his
remarkable technique in bringing to life the objects on
the canvas. There were several landscapes done at Sweet
Waters, but, in particular, she liked the one of her gabled
home with the rugged mountains towering towards the
sky in the background. Her glance was inevitably drawn
towards a painting of the waterfall with the crystal clear
waters of the pool in the foreground. It was so alive
that she could almost hear the roar of the water, but
bitter-sweet memories tore through her insides, and she
turned away abruptly to admire instead a miniature of
the fast-moving stream where his caravan had stood
sheltered beneath the willow trees.

His work was outstanding, but she would have found
it a more enjoyable experience had she not been so aware
of his silent observation.

'What do you think?' he asked at length, and she could no longer avoid acknowledging his presence.

'I think they're excellent,' she replied with an enthusiasm she could not quite suppress, 'and it's quite obvious why the critics are raving about your work.'

'Come this way,' he said abruptly without commenting on her praise, and took her arm to guide her towards the opposite end of the room where a large painting stood propped up against the wall in the corner. It was draped with a canvas cloth, and, when Abbey glanced at him curiously, he said: 'I promised you that you would see your portrait before anyone else, didn't I?'

Her heart skipped a beat as she looked up at him. 'You remembered?'

'I seldom forget a promise,' he told her, his mouth curving in that cynical smile she remembered so well as he lifted the portrait on to a vacant stand.

'What would you have done if I hadn't been here this evening?' she asked, holding her breath for some reason.

'The portrait would not have been exhibited,' he replied harshly, igniting a little spark of joy in her heart, then he gestured abruptly with his hand. 'Stand back a little,' he ordered.

Abbey did as she was told, and with one sweeping movement Hammond removed the covering to reveal the almost life-size portrait of herself. Abbey stared at it, and felt her breath lock in her throat. She saw the face she encountered each day in the mirror, but there was a subtle difference to it which she could not quite explain to herself.

She was seated on a rock with her hair trailing across one shoulder, and he had draped her body in a diaphanous garment which concealed, but did not quite hide the shapely curves of her youthful figure, and his magical brush had given her the appearance of a mythical, mysterious being. Hidden in the depths of her sapphire blue eyes there was a mixture of tender humour, uncertainty, and a yearning for something she neither knew, nor understood. And that, Abbey realised in dismay, was exactly how she had felt on those first few occasions when she had sat for Hammond.

'Well?' he demanded abruptly, observing the expressions flitting across her sensitive face with a hint of sardonic humour in his eyes.

'It . . . it's beautiful,' she murmured haltingly, unable to think of anything she could add which would express her disturbed feelings at that moment.

'I told you you were beautiful, didn't I?'

'Do I . . . do I really look like that?' she asked in a hushed voice while she took another long, critical look at the portrait.

'I painted you as I saw you then.'

Something in the way he spoke made her shiver as if an icy breeze had wafted up against her, and her fingers tightened on the clasp of her purse in an effort to steady them. 'Is it for sale?'

'It is, until further notice, my property.' Their eyes met, but Abbey could not sustain his probing glance. 'Is Derek here with you?'

For the second time that evening she heard herself saying, 'I came alone.'

His gaze swept down to her ringless fingers, and she felt more than just a little bewildered when he demanded harshly, 'When are you going to marry him?'

'I'm not going to marry Derek. At least . . .' She paused, biting her lip in uncertainty and confusion, then she tried again. 'He has asked me to, but . . .'

'Didn't I tell you once that you don't know your own

mind?' he mocked her ruthlessly, and she turned away to hide the pain in her eyes.

'Why did you leave the farm so unexpectedly, and without even saying goodbye?' she asked the question which had disturbed her so intensely these past months, and steeled herself subconsciously for the painful truth long before Hammond started to speak.

'Your mother told me that your father had taken you to Durban to settle the problems between Derek and yourself. She told me you'd decided to marry him after all, and that she would consider it a favour if I was gone from Sweet Waters before you returned home that afternoon.'

His words shattered every other theory she had had on the matter, and, as it hammered home the painfully distressing truth, she went almost as white as his lacy shirt-front.

'Oh, my God!' she whispered hoarsely, trying to assimilate the shock of knowing that her mother had been responsible for these months of agony she had had to endure.

'I'm damned if I know why you couldn't have told me yourself,' Hammond's voice continued to lash her. 'I thought we'd reached the stage where we would be completely honest with each other, but that just shows how wrong one can be.'

Abbey felt like weeping as she stared a long way up into his granite-hard face, but she swallowed convulsively and made an attempt to explain. 'Hammond, I didn't——'

'The doors are opening,' he stopped her abruptly, and she turned to see the people filtering swiftly into the hall. 'We'll talk again later,' Hammond said behind her, and then he was walking away from her to speak to an elderly, bearded man who was obviously of some importance.

Abbey caught sight of her parents and made her way towards them. Her mother looked tense and strangely pale, and Abbey was beginning to understand why. She had behaved despicably, and Abbey would tell her so at the first available opportunity.

A hush fell upon the crowd as the man Hammond had spoken to stepped on to the rostrum at the far end of the room, and Abbey glanced enquiringly at her father.

'That's Professor Yates,' Edward informed her after consulting his programme. 'He lectures in art at the University, I believe.'

'Ladies and gentlemen,' the Professor began, capturing the attention of the expectant crowd, 'it gives me great pleasure this evening to introduce the work of an ex-student of mine, Hammond Scott-Gordon. He has excelled himself as director and chairman of Gordon's, which you all know as an exclusive chain store throughout the country, but after what I have glimpsed here this evening, I find myself wishing that he would spend more time at the easel instead of his desk.'

Nothing registered with Abbey after the initial shock of learning the truth about Hammond. Gordon's was one of the largest companies of its kind in the country, and the discovery that Hammond was the head of this firm was a blow that left her momentarily stunned until she realised how totally she had been deceived.

'Oh, my goodness!' Claire whispered agitatedly, pressing a scented handkerchief to her nose and leaning heavily on her father's arm as if she was in danger of fainting. 'Abbey ... if only I'd known!'

With a combination of disappointment and fury, Abbey turned on her mother with an icy cynicism in her voice. 'I'm sure it makes all the difference in the world to you now that you know who and what he really is, but, thanks to your interference, I'm happy to tell you that it's too late.'

'What are the two of you muttering about?' her father demanded.

'Ask Mother!' Abbey whispered furiously, her hands clutching her evening purse so tightly that her fingers ached. 'Let *her* tell you the reason why Hammond left the farm in such a hurry!'

'Claire?' her father frowned down at her mother questioningly.

As Abbey walked away from them she heard her mother say unsteadily, 'I—I did it for Abbey. I didn't know——'

Abbey did not wait to hear more, she was too busy making her way towards the exit, and a deep-seated anger was beginning to surge through her, giving her the strength to walk out of the building and along the busy street to the Morningside Hotel.

She had been grossly deceived, she told herself later as she paced about in her room like a caged animal seeking an outlet. She had imagined Hammond to be a man of insubstantial means, and he had encouraged her to think of him in that way. It had been a foul thing to do; making her believe that, like herself, he looked upon her mother's wealthy, prejudiced friends with as much contempt as she did, and all the time he very cleverly hid the fact that he was one of them.

'Well, Mr Hammond Scott-Gordon,' she addressed his imaginary presence furiously, 'you can go to the devil for all I care!'

She walked quickly towards the telephone and lifted the receiver. The girl at reception answered instantly, and Abbey asked her if she would telephone the airport in order to alter her return flight to Durban. She wanted to leave as early as possible the following morning, and she was determined not to remain in Johannesburg a minute longer than she had to.

She dropped the receiver on to its cradle, then pulled the pins from her hair in an agitated manner until it cascaded down to her shoulders in a thick, wavy curtain which accentuated the paleness of her thin features, but, as she flung the pins on to the dressing table, her vision blurred with tears. An exclamation of disgust was on her lips. She despised herself for her weakness and, dashing away her tears impatiently, pulled her suitcase out from under the bed.

The telephone rang shrilly some minutes later and, turning away from the suitcase on the bed, she crossed the room to answer it.

'I've reserved a seat for you on the eight-fifteen flight to Durban tomorrow morning,' the girl at reception informed her briskly. 'I hope that meets with your approval, Miss Mitchell?'

'That suits me perfectly,' Abbey told her hastily before she replaced the receiver, 'and thank you very much for your trouble.'

'It's over and done with,' she muttered to herself when she flung open the doors of the wardrobe. She would have to leave the hotel very early in the morning. That meant that she would have to pack her suitcase before she could think of going to bed that evening, but she blessed the fact that she had something to do.

She was startled, minutes later, by a knock on her door and, pausing in the act of folding up one of her dresses, she asked hesitantly, 'Who is it?'

'Hammond,' that clear, deep voice sent little shock waves along her nervous system. 'Open the door—I want to speak to you.'

There was a loud drumming against her temples when,

after a moment of indecision, she crossed the room and turned the key in the lock. The door swung open under his impatient hand before she could touch the handle, and she stood there in the dimly lit room, a slim wand of a girl, hollow-eyed, and mentally stripped of her veneer of sophistication and confidence. She not only felt vulnerable, but was certain she looked it as he stepped into the room and closed the door firmly behind him, and the only thing she had left to cling to was her bitterness and anger.

'What are you doing here?' she demanded coldly. 'Why aren't you at the exhibition?'

'Why did you run away?' he counter-questioned harshly, giving her the peculiar feeling that she was being threatened.

'I didn't run,' she evaded his question sarcastically, raising her chin in a gesture of defiance. 'I walked out quite calmly.'

'Don't act clever with me, Abbey!' he said bitingly, crowding the small room with his austere presence, but she was not going to be intimidated by him.

'I'm most dreadfully sorry,' she continued with mock servility. 'Please do tell me how I'm supposed to act in the presence of the revered director and chairman of Gordon's.'

The air crackled with tension between them, and during the ensuing silence she suspected that she had gone too far, but his voice was surprisingly calm when he said: 'I never asked for the position I hold. I was primed for it from the day my uncle took my sister and me into his home. My uncle was a hard man in every way, but he'll always have my gratitude for making me what I am today.'

'Your explanation has come a little too late.'

'You have every reason to be annoyed,' he agreed

grimly, 'but I give you my word that I had every intention of telling you the truth about myself.'

There was a touch of bitter cynicism in the smile Abbey slanted up at him. 'Do you expect me to believe you?'

'Abbey, I'd like to explain,' he began, the deep timbre of his voice vibrating along her receptive nerves, but she evaded his hands, and turned away from him to hide the tears which had leapt into her eyes.

'What fun you must have had, laughing up your sleeve at us all for believing you to be a wretchedly poor artist, while all the time you're so wealthy that I don't doubt you could have bought Sweet Waters, along with quite a few other farms in the district, without so much as denting your bank balance.' She laughed mirthlessly as she added: 'You certainly succeeded in deceiving us, but, unlike yourself, I'm not amused by it.'

She turned towards her bed and pushed the partially folded dress into the suitcase with more vigour than was necessary.

'What are you doing?' Hammond demanded coldly.

'I'm packing,' she snapped, aware of his eyes following every move she made. 'I'm returning to Durban on the early morning flight.'

'You're not going anywhere!' he thundered at her, and he was beside her in a flash, taking her suitcase and flinging it, contents and all, on to the floor so that her clothes spilled out in an untidy heap.

'How dare you!' she almost screamed at him, her blue eyes blazing with an inner fury at the thought of what a fool she had been.

'I dare, because you and I have a great deal of unfinished business to attend to before I'll allow you to return to Durban—*if* I'll allow you to return, that is.'

He was so close to her now that her nerves vibrated

with his disturbing nearness. The familiar smell of his masculine cologne attacked her senses, but she was too infuriated to allow herself to be swayed by her emotions.

'I shall leave when I please,' she informed him coldly, 'and as far as I'm concerned, we have nothing further to discuss with each other.'

'Oh, yes, we have,' he barked at her, taking her roughly by the shoulders and swinging her round to face him. 'What does Derek mean to you?'

'At this very moment a damn sight more than you do,' she snapped, trying unsuccessfully to free herself from those fingers biting so cruelly into her flesh.

'Are you going to marry him?'

'That's none of your business!'

'Damn you, Abbey! Tell me the truth, or do I have to force it out of you?' Hammond's hands tightened on her shoulders, and his touch was a sweet agony which she knew she dared not surrender to as she found herself staring up into his stern face. 'Are you going to marry Derek?'

His eyes were slits of green fire burning down into hers, demanding the truth which she was equally determined not to give. She had humiliated herself enough in the past, and she was determined not to do so again.

'I might marry him,' she said at length.

'Do you love him?'

'That's a personal matter between Derek and myself, and I refuse to discuss it with you,' she replied cuttingly, and had the satisfaction of seeing him wince.

'Perhaps you'll answer this,' he continued, releasing her so abruptly that she almost stumbled. 'Do you love me?'

'*No!*' she spat out the word fiercely, but everything within her cried out the opposite as her angry glance swept him from head to foot, taking in the expensive linen of his suit, the fine silk of his shirt, and the polished leather of his shoes. 'I don't know you. You're a stranger to me, and I don't very much like what I see.' She saw him take a gold cigarette case out of his jacket pocket, he snapped it open, selected a cigarette, and lit it, but before he could return the case to his pocket she gestured towards it disparagingly. 'Not even *that* looks familiar when I think of the crushed packet of cigarettes you always carried about with you.'

He frowned down at the cigarette between his fingers, and said derisively, 'I'm still the same underneath all this fancy gear.'

'Are you?'

'Clothes don't necessarily make the man, Abbey,' he reminded her with a touch of the old mockery. 'I'm still the same man I always was. I enjoy my wealth for the simple reason that it gives me the freedom to travel the country whenever I have the opportunity, and during my travels I usually do what I find pleases me most— painting. I'm not ashamed of what I have, and I don't look down on others who have less.' He drew hard on his cigarette and exhaled the smoke forcibly through his nose as he crossed the room to stand at the open window with his broad, formidable back turned towards her. 'That's what I liked about you. It didn't matter to you who or what I was, and it was a welcome relief from the women who wanted me solely for my wealth and position in society. Can you blame me for wanting to revel in the situation for as long as possible?'

'That's very touching,' she remarked, hardening her heart to the plea in his voice, 'but it's too late. I was honest with you, and I expected honesty in return, but all I got from you was lies and deceit.'

There was a prolonged, strained silence before he

turned to face her, and his eyes were glittering strangely when they met hers. 'You said it was too late. What, exactly, do you mean by that?'

She turned from him to hide the tell-tale trembling of her lips, and was surprised to hear herself say in a controlled voice, 'It's too late to salvage anything between us. I have no further interest in you, and I hope we never have to see each other again.'

Abbey felt as if she was being torn apart by the conflicting emotions raging within her. Her heart said: 'Don't be a fool! Don't throw away the only chance you have left!' But her mind argued: Let him return to Shelagh Varney and their 'near perfect' relationship. Shelagh knew him for what he was. There had been no secrets between them; no lies and deceit, and there would be no need to adapt to someone who had all at once become such a total stranger.

'Please go, and leave me alone,' she begged in a hoarse whisper, pressing her fingers against her throbbing temples, and moments later she heard the door closing behind him.

Without Hammond's vital presence to breathe life into the small hotel room, Abbey found it bleak and empty, and she choked back a sob in a determined effort not to cry. She had shed enough tears during these past months, and she was certainly not going to shed another tear for someone as undeserving as Hammond.

She picked up her suitcase and rescued her clothes off the floor where Hammond had flung them, then resumed her packing in earnest. She would be returning to Durban in the morning, and she had made up her mind at last to marry Derek. He had always been honest with her. She knew what he was and, above all, she knew that she could trust him. Derek might be dominating, prejudiced and overbearing at times, but he had made no secret of it. She would always know where she stood with him—and to the devil with the rest. What did it matter that she did not love him? She was fond of him, and she respected him. Love would come later and, in time, she might even discover that she had made a wise decision.

Derek . . . dear, sweet Derek. He loved her, and at this moment he was waiting anxiously for her to return to him with an answer to his proposal, and she was not going to disappoint him a second time. He would receive the answer he was hoping for, she decided, silencing the urgent voice of her heart. She had listened to her heart once before, and it had led to humiliation, heartache and despair. She was not going to go through it all again. Not for anyone. Not even for Hammond.

CHAPTER TEN

IT was late that evening when Abbey emerged from the bathroom, and she hastily fastened the belt of her silk robe about her waist when there was a knock on her door. Her father's voice replied to her anxious query, and her small, rounded jaw was set with determination when she opened the door to admit her parents.

'We have something to say to you, Abbey,' her father announced sternly and, glancing at her mother, he added meaningfully, 'Don't we, Claire?'

'Yes, Edward,' her mother agreed in an uncommonly subdued manner as she faced Abbey with a look of appeal in her grey eyes. 'I admit that when you and your father were away from the farm I made use of the opportunity to see to it that Mr Scott-Gordon would be gone before you returned. I did it because I was concerned for your sake, and because I believed you were being influenced by a man who had nothing to offer you except a nomadic existence with very little of the comforts you were accustomed to. I was so certain that you loved Derek, you see, and I was only doing what I considered was best for you, but I—I realise now how wrong I'd been, and I owe you an apology.'

'You owe me nothing, Mother,' Abbey replied, and her cold, detached voice sounded as if it belonged to someone else. 'You wanted me to marry Derek, and that's exactly what I'm going to do.'

Claire looked horrified. 'Oh, no, you can't!'

'Oh, yes, I can, and I *am*,' Abbey insisted, a cynical smile curving her beautiful mouth.

'But what about Mr Scott-Gordon?'

'What about him?' Abbey demanded abruptly.

'But——' Claire shook her head helplessly. 'I don't understand.'

'Abbey,' her father intervened at this point, 'you love Hammond, don't you?'

'I loved the man who came to my engagement party in denims because he didn't possess such a thing as an evening suit,' she corrected, despising herself for the tremor in her voice. 'He had nothing, and never claimed to have anything other than that battered old jeep and cumbersome caravan. Like myself, he despised those who considered wealth and status the most important attribute, but I discovered this evening that he'd deceived me all along.' She paused to draw breath, and swallowed convulsively. 'I don't know this man we met this evening, and I couldn't have discovered in a more brutal way exactly how little I really knew about him. Hammond Scott-Gordon is a stranger to me, but I do know that he's damned good at lies and deceit.'

'Aren't you being a little harsh in your judgement, my girl?' her father cautioned her.

'No harsher than he was to conceal the truth from me,' she replied stubbornly, but there was an unmistakable note of anguish in her voice as she added: 'Don't you see? If he couldn't trust me with the truth about himself, then how can I believe that he thought anything of me at all?'

'I can understand that,' her father nodded, placing a heavy hand on her shoulder, 'but you're angry now, and perhaps a little confused. When you've simmered down and had time to think you may see it all differently, and then it may be too late.'

'It's already too late.'

'What do you mean?'

Abbey turned away from the two people watching her so intently and walked across the room towards the dressing table. She picked up her brush and tapped it restlessly against her open palm, then she put it down again, and turned to face them with some of her earlier determination mirrored in her fine features. 'I've made up my mind to marry Derek, and nothing is going to change that.'

A sharp knock on the door interrupted the strained silence, and Abbey jumped nervously. Something close to fear clutched at her throat and, at her silent gesture, her father went to the door and opened it.

Hammond stepped into the room, a tall, broad-shouldered, frightening stranger with the stamp of wealth all over him. Her mind rejected him, but her heart throbbed wildly in her breast when his eyes met hers across the room.

'I'd like to speak to Abbey alone, if you don't mind,' he announced with no more than a brief glance in her parents' direction.

'But *I* mind!' she exclaimed sharply, gesturing her parents to stay. 'We have nothing more to say to each other!'

Hammond ignored her and, turning to face Edward and Claire, he repeated his request in an infuriatingly calm manner. 'Will you leave us, please?'

'You have no right to come in here and order my parents out of my room without my permission,' she almost shouted at him.

'Be quiet!' he ordered with an unexpected savagery that drove every vestige of colour from her face, and it also made her father take her mother by the arm to usher her quickly from the room.

'There are a few matters you and I have to discuss,' Hammond announced the moment they were alone, 'and you were obviously not in a mood to think or speak rationally when I was here earlier.'

'I was in a perfectly rational mood, just as I am now,' Abbey argued furiously, but her legs felt curiously like jelly beneath her.

'You're shaking,' he said abruptly. 'I suggest you sit down before you fall down.'

'The hell I will!' she shouted.

'Sit down!' he ordered harshly, taking her roughly by the shoulders and pushing her down on to the bed.

'How dare you come in here and treat me in this abominable manner?' she demanded huskily, and more than a little frightened now. 'I'm not one of your puppets in the Gordon's network who'll dance whenever you care to pull the string!'

'Shut up!' His eyes blazed down into hers. 'There are certain things you ought to know, and I don't want to waste unnecessary time.'

She looked away from him, unable to sustain his glance for fear of weakening and allowing him to see too much. 'I don't think there's anything you could tell me that would interest me in the least.'

'I've cancelled your flight to Durban.'

'You've *what*?' she demanded incredulously, her glance sweeping upwards to meet his, and she encountered that familiar mocking smile which so often had curved his mouth. 'How dare you do such a thing?'

'I thought that would interest you.'

'You're despicable!' she hissed up at him, her eyes darkening with fury. 'You had no right to——'

'I had every right,' he interrupted arrogantly, silencing her with an imperious wave of his hand, then his razor-sharp glance raked over her, taking in the agitated rise and fall of her breasts, and the angry flush on her cheeks. 'What have you got on under that thing?'

'Nothing,' she snapped without thinking, and a shiver of apprehension raced up her spine when his smile deepened.

'How delightful,' he murmured, and before she could guess his intentions she was jerked up into his arms and imprisoned against the hard length of his immaculately clad body.

'Let me go, you fiend!' she cried frantically, beating her clenched fists against his chest, but he was as immovable as a rock.

'There's only one way I can think of to bring you to your senses,' he said, the strength of his arms almost crushing the breath from her body, and as her lips parted to berate him, his mouth came down on to hers with a bruising force, demanding her submission.

Abbey tried desperately not to respond, to remain passive beneath this onslaught on her emotions, but her heart was beating so fast that it almost choked her, and a wild surge of ecstasy swept through her like a tornado, rendering her helpless in the wake of it.

It was a long time before Hammond released her, and when he did she was shaking so much that she had to sit down for fear of collapsing in a heap at his feet.

'Are you ready to talk sensibly?' he demanded in a dangerously soft voice, and she stared up at him reproachfully while she fingered her bruised lips.

'You shouldn't have done that.'

His jaw hardened as he towered over her menacingly. 'For God's sake, Abbey, don't you realise how important it is for us to talk this thing out?'

She stared up at him with a bewildered look in her eyes, not quite knowing what to say, or what to do, then she sighed and gestured vaguely towards the vacant bed alongside her own. 'If—if we're going to talk, then I—I suggest you sit down over there before I get a crick in my neck.'

'Would you mind very much if I made myself comfortable?' he asked tersely and, not waiting for her to reply, he took off his jacket and bow tie and unbuttoned his shirt, giving her more than just a glimpse of his tanned, hair-roughened chest. 'We owe each other an explanation,' he said at length, hitching up his pants and seating himself on the bed facing her. 'Shall I start, or will you?'

The desire to touch him was like a hollow ache at the pit of her stomach, and she swallowed nervously. 'You make this all sound so cold-blooded.'

'Abbey,' he sighed exasperatedly, 'we both have a lot of explaining to do, and if I don't behave in this cold-blooded manner, then I'm damned certain I'll be making love to you instead of trying to make some sense out of this whole wretched situation.'

Her hands fluttered in her lap, and she clasped them together tightly, but there was nothing she could do about the flush that stained her cheeks. The memory of intimacies shared rushed to the surface of her mind, and her body tingled as if from a physical caress. She was vulnerable and so desperately afraid, but her resentment crumbled, and she knew that she could no longer withhold the truth from him.

'There's something I must tell you,' she said when she managed to find her voice.

'Good, we're getting somewhere,' Hammond sighed audibly. 'What is it that you must tell me?'

'My mother lied to you,' she began unsteadily, unable to meet his eyes. 'I never went to Durban to see or speak to Derek. My father had business to attend to in Pietermaritzburg, and I went along to keep him company.'

The ensuing silence was almost deafening, a horn blared loudly somewhere in the street below her window, and her nerves were still quivering protestingly when Hammond demanded incredulously, 'You were where, did you say?'

'I was in Pietermaritzburg with my father,' she repeated, her face controlled and outwardly calm as she looked up to meet the onslaught of his eyes. 'It was only after I learnt of your sudden departure that I returned to Durban.'

Hammond's jaw hardened. 'To pick up where you left off with Derek?'

'To try and make something of the mess my life had become,' she corrected, sustaining his probing glance for what seemed like an eternity.

'When your mother told me that you'd decided to marry Derek I had no reason to disbelieve her.'

'You had *every* reason to disbelieve her! I ... oh, God!' Her control snapped and she buried her quivering face in her hands so that her voice was muffled when she said in an agonised voice, 'I did everything except hand myself to you on a platter, and when I arrived home that evening to find you'd gone without a word I—I felt like dying.'

'Abbey?' His fingers were like steel bands clamped about her wrists as he drew her hands away from her white face, but the eyes that met his were dull with the memory of her suffering. 'Are you telling me that you love me?'

She shook her head, and looked away to hide the trembling of her lips. 'I'm telling you what I felt then.'

'To hell with what you felt *then*!' he announced savagely, releasing her wrists to push his fingers through his hair in an unusually agitated manner. 'It's what you feel *now* that's of importance to me!'

'Why is it important?' she asked a little breathlessly, her skin still tingling where his fingers had bit into the flesh.

'It's important because I happen to love you.'

Abbey stared at him, joy and disbelief fighting for supremacy, but she dared not lower her guard and lay herself open to more pain and misery.

'Heaven knows I'd like to believe you, but you've never given me any reason to,' she whispered accusingly, but her heart leapt wildly in her throat when he crossed the space between the beds and sat down beside her. His thigh was hard against her own, and his hand was beneath her chin, forcing her to meet the probing intensity of his glance.

'I've loved you from the first moment I saw you, Abbey, but I couldn't risk telling you until I was more sure of you.'

She desperately wanted to believe him, but she was too wary of being hurt again, and her voice was trite when she said: 'Correct me if I'm wrong, but I believe I told you quite plainly on two different occasions how I felt about you.'

'How could I be sure of someone who was up in the clouds about her engagement one minute, and breaking it off the next?' he accused grimly, releasing her and pushing his fingers through his hair once more so that it fell across his forehead in that old familiar way. 'You had all the damn symptoms of someone who didn't know her own mind, and I was determined not to say anything until I was convinced that you felt the same way I did.'

'I never loved Derek,' she explained quietly. 'I imagined that what I felt for him was love, but I never really knew what love was until I met you.'

'Abbey?' he questioned, his eyes searching hers intently for the truth, but she was not yet ready to allow him to see into the sanctum of her heart.

'What about Shelagh Varney?' she asked. 'You said you cared for her.'

'I said I cared for her in a manner of speaking, if you remember,' he reminded her with a derisive smile. 'She's my secretary, I pay her salary, and in that way I suppose one could say I care for her.'

Relief washed over her like a soothing balm, but she was not quite satisfied. 'She arrived with you at the exhibition this evening, and she looked terribly possessive clinging to your arm in the way she did.'

'When you stop to consider that she practically organised the entire show for me, then it was only fair that she accompanied me to the exhibition, and as for the latter, I would imagine most secretaries are possessive to a degree about their bosses.'

Abbey lowered her eyes before his mocking gaze. 'Is she your part-time mistress as well?'

'Don't be ridiculous!' His eyes burned into hers as he took her by the shoulders in a punishing grip and shook her. 'When Shelagh came to Sweet Waters it was in the company car, and with urgent papers that needed my signature. There were certain business matters which had to be discussed, but in the end it became clear to me that I would have to come here to Johannesburg personally to sort out the problems which had arisen, and that's where I was that weekend, here in my office, working like the very devil so that I could get back to you as soon as possible.'

'And all you got for your trouble was the stinging end of my riding crop across your cheek,' she groaned, her eyes filling with tears as she recalled her unforgivable action. 'I wish you'd told me all this before.'

Hammond pulled her roughly into his arms, and she buried her face against his shoulder, loving the familiar smell of his masculine cologne while she spilled tears all over his expensive silk shirt.

'I almost told you everything that morning after your last sitting. I considered it very strongly, but I wasn't quite sure how you would take it,' Hammond confessed, his voice vibrantly low as he brushed her hair away from her face, and showered tantalising little kisses on to her closed eyelids and damp cheeks. 'When your mother told me the following morning that you'd decided to marry Derek, I thought it was just as well I'd remained silent.' She felt the swift rise and fall of his chest beneath her hand, then he said savagely, 'My God, I would have killed you that morning if I could have lain my hands on you!'

'Hammond . . .' she whispered his name unsteadily, her voice muffled against his shoulder. 'Oh, Hammond, I tried so desperately to forget you, but these past three months have been sheer hell!'

'You don't need to tell me that,' he groaned, his arms tightening about her almost convulsively. 'I spent my days and nights imagining you married to Derek, and it very nearly drove me insane.'

He prised her face out into the open, his eyes on the hollows and planes of her tear-stained face, then he plundered her lips with a hunger that matched her own, and she clung to him, her fingers gripping his wide shoulders as if to reassure herself that he was not part of a dream which would vanish the next minute. But this was no dream, she realised when she felt his hands moving urgently against her back, their heat penetrating the silk of her robe, and awakening emotions which had lain dormant for months.

There was an element of danger in the situation and, with her hands against his chest, she eased her lips from his and leaned away from him.

'There's something else I must tell you,' she began hesitantly, and her pulse rate was a little too high for comfort. 'Derek asked me to marry him, and I told him I'd give him my answer on my return to Durban.'

'Like hell you'll marry him!' Hammond almost shouted at her, his eyes blazing down into hers like twin fires intent upon devouring her, and a grimness settling about his mouth. 'You're going to marry me, and no one else,' he stated harshly and, for a moment, Abbey felt almost faint with happiness.

'Are you asking me, or telling me?' she smiled tremulously, trailing her fingers lightly along the side of his rigid jaw.

'I'm asking you,' he said, capturing her hand and pressing his lips against her palm while his eyes looked into hers with a tenderness that made her want to weep for joy. 'Will you marry me?'

'Yes,' she whispered urgently, her eyes sparkling with happy tears, and her face radiant with a love which seemed to burst the banks of her hungry heart. 'Oh, yes, please!'

She heard him draw a sharp breath, and her soft mules slipped off her feet as he swung her legs on to the bed and lifted her higher up against the pillows so that her hair was spread out in a dark, lustrous halo about her face. He followed her down, giving her no time to think, and they kissed with a hungry, searing passion which the months of needless separation had intensified. Abbey trembled against him, and he instantly drew her closer, making her aware of his need as well as her own. Her mind warned her to take care, but her body had a will of its own, and she responded with an eager warmth as his lips trailed a fiery path down to the opening of her robe where her pulse was beating erratically. Knowing that he loved her was like a heady wine, and her fingers tore impatiently at his shirt buttons in her desire to feel the hair-roughened warmth of his muscled flesh against her soft palms. She unashamedly took the lead as her emotions clamoured for an outlet, and it was only when she felt him tremble against her that she was made aware of his effort to curb his desire. His hand tightened unexpectedly in a punishing grip on her hip, and when he raised his head she saw the tiny beads of perspiration which had gathered on his forehead. There was naked desire in his peculiar eyes, and the strain of controlling it made his rugged features look grim and drawn.

'Do you have any idea what it's doing to me to hold you like this and know that you have nothing on except this flimsy thing?' he grunted, trailing an erotic finger from her throat down to where her robe had parted to reveal the creamy curve of her breasts, and a thousand little nerves came alive to his touch when his hand dipped beneath the silk in a sensually arousing caress.

'I love you, Hammond,' she whispered, her eyes luminous, and the pupils enlarged with the extent of her emotions.

'Don't look at me like that, woman,' he warned thickly, his voice a low growl in her ears as his lips raked the sensitive cord of her throat. 'I've never wanted or thought I could want anyone as much as I want you at this moment, and the temptation to make love to you is unbearably strong.'

An intense longing pulsated through her and, driven on by an aching need she could not even explain to herself, she confessed haltingly, 'I know I ought to—tell you to go, but I—I don't think I could bear it if you—left me now.'

He drew away from her slightly, his hand sliding from her breast to her throat where her pulse throbbed wildly, and there was a frightening little silence before he demanded hoarsely, 'Do you know what you're saying, Abbey?'

He was, surprisingly, giving her time to reconsider her actions, but the weeks and months of desolation and despair dictated her answer. 'Yes, I know what I'm saying.'

His eyes darkened to a smouldering green fire, and Abbey was amazed to discover that his hand was shaking as he lifted a strand of dark, silky hair away from her flushed cheek. 'You want me to stay?'

'Yes,' she croaked, tears of happiness glittering in her eyes as she locked her arms about his neck. 'Heaven help me, but I do!'

'Abbey,' he murmured in a voice vibrant with emotion, and it was like a velvety caress touching her very soul. He kissed away her tears, and tenderly, almost reverently, he whispered, 'My sweet, adorable Abbey!'

For a long time he seemed content merely to hold her, his caresses comforting rather than arousing, his kisses reassuring rather than sensual, but desire cannot be withheld for ever, and when he finally made love to her she was a willing and eager partner in the act of uniting mind, soul, and body.

Later, when Hammond lay asleep beside her in the darkness with his shoulder acting as a pillow for her head, she nestled closer to him on the narrow bed and

sighed contentedly. He had made love to her with such
tender concern for her innocence that she had not
known one moment of fear, only a surging tide of the
most incredible happiness and pleasure which had driven
her to the peak of desire and beyond. She had been swept
along into a world of the most indescribable ecstasy, and
she had emerged a woman in the fullest sense; a woman
who loved and who knew she was loved in return.

She felt no shame when she thought of the intimacies
they had shared; she felt elated, and filled with such
intense happiness that she felt like weeping, but instead
she closed her eyes and, for the first time in months,
went to sleep with a smile on her lips.

Abbey awakened early the following morning and,
taking care not to disturb Hammond, she slipped out of
bed and pulled on her robe, fastening the belt as she
padded barefoot into the bathroom. When a tray of
coffee was brought up to her room, she was dressed and
ready to take it at the door. There was only one cup on
the tray, but there was enough coffee in the pot for two,
she discovered, a mischievous smile lifting the corners
of her mouth as she placed the tray on the dressing
table. She wondered vaguely what the management
would say if they should discover that Hammond had
stayed the night, but she was too happy to give it much
thought as she poured Hammond's coffee the way she
knew he liked it.

Loath to wake him, Abbey placed his coffee very
carefully on the small cupboard between the beds. He
looked extraordinarily relaxed, and considerably
younger in his sleep. His rugged, often harsh features
looked oddly vulnerable, and a shadowy growth of
beard was clearly visible on his lean cheeks and square,
dented jaw. She had never seen him unshaven before,

but she decided at once that she liked what she saw. His hair lay untidily across his forehead, and, with the sheet covering him only from his hips down, the wide expanse of his hair-roughened chest was exposed to her glance. He looked so achingly familiar this morning, and a tender smile lit her eyes as she stared down at the man she had fallen so desperately in love with all those months ago.

The man she had met at the exhibition the previous evening was still a stranger to her, and someone she would yet have to become acquainted with, but she no longer feared the prospect. She looked forward to the adventure of discovering every facet of this man's character, and her love for him flowed from her fingertips as she brushed his hair away from his forehead.

His eyelids flickered, and it was a new experience to find herself staring down into the glittering depths of his sleep-filled eyes. His glance was mocking, yet tender, but when that familiar warmth stole into her cheeks his hand found hers and, responding to that persuasive tug, she sat down on the bed beside him.

'You'll have to marry me now,' he told her with a suggestion of triumph in his smile.

'I'm not putting up an argument,' she assured him, her eyes sparkling with humour.

His hands slid beneath her hair at the nape of her neck, and he drew her head down to his. 'I'll make arrangements for us to be married this morning.'

'I'd like that,' she whispered against his lips, and for a time his kisses transported her into that world where only he could take her, but disturbing thoughts crowded her mind, and temporarily clouded her happiness.

'What is it?' he asked abruptly when he sensed her withdrawal, and a frown creased his brow as he released her and pushed himself up against the pillows.

'I have a job from which I'm supposed to resign. I can't

simply walk out on them,' she explained in a troubled voice as she handed him his coffee. 'And there's Derek, too.'

'If you'll give me your employer's home telephone number, then I'll settle that problem for you with very little effort,' Hammond stated with the arrogance of one in a position to manipulate others. 'And as for Derek, I——'

'I'll give him a ring and speak to him personally,' she interrupted adamantly.

His mouth tightened ominously. 'Is that really necessary?'

'Yes, it is,' she insisted, revelling in that spark of jealousy in his eyes, but determined to do what she considered her duty. 'Derek has been very kind to me, and his friendship meant a lot to me during these past months. He asked me to marry him, and I owe him an answer—even if it's a negative one.'

The silence between them was strained while Hammond drank his coffee, but when he placed his empty cup on the cupboard beside the bed, he said grudgingly, 'You're right, of course. You owe him the courtesy of a personal call.'

Abbey poured herself a cup of coffee while Hammond went through to the bathroom, and that left her with plenty of time to think. When he emerged half an hour later, dressed only in the trousers of his dark evening suit, he fingered his chin ruefully.

'I need a shave,' he grunted humorously, but his mouth twisted derisively when he met her unsmiling glance. 'You haven't changed your mind about marrying me, have you?'

Abbey looked startled for a moment, then a smile quivered on her lips. 'I was thinking that we shall have to tell my parents of our decision, and . . .' a look of bitterness crept into her eyes, '. . . my mother will be thrilled, of course. You're exactly the sort of son-in-law she's always wanted.'

'Don't torture yourself with bitterness, my darling,' he said, pausing in the act of putting on his shirt. 'The only thing that matters is that it all worked out for the best in the end.'

'That's true, I suppose,' she admitted gravely, watching him fasten the buttons of his shirt before he pushed the ends into his pants.

Hammond looked at her strangely, and during the ensuing silence she sensed a growing tension between them which she could not understand.

'You don't regret last night, do you?'

'No!' she replied at once, her eyes wide and startled, then she asked a little warily, 'Do you?'

'Abbey, love of my life!' he laughed suddenly, opening his arms wide and invitingly. 'Come here and take your punishment for asking such a silly question,' he instructed, and she obeyed with a choked laugh to lose herself in his crushing embrace. His beard was rough against her skin, but she was too wildly happy to care as she surrendered herself to his kisses, and melted beneath his sensual caresses until her blood flowed like molten fire through her veins.

There was a note of warning in the deep timbre of his voice when his lips left hers to explore the sensitive areas at the base of her throat. 'I love you, Abbey, and what I have, I hold,' he said, his hands sliding possessively over her hips as he drew her closer into the curve of his body. 'Nothing, except death, shall ever part us again, and you might as well accept that as fact.'

Abbey could not fault his statement. It was what she wanted more than anything else on earth; to belong to Hammond completely, and to know that he belonged to her. Nothing else mattered, and bitter-sweet memories faded, leaving only the sweet joy of a future with the man she loved at her side.

Harlequin® Plus

A WORD ABOUT THE AUTHOR

Yvonne Whittal grew up in South Africa, spending her summers on the coast and her winter months inland at a sheep farm in the Karoo region. It was there that Yvonne came to know the farmers who loved the earth and faced a never ending struggle for survival. Her first novel, *East to Barryvale* (Romance #1915, published in 1975), was inspired by the people of the area.

Yvonne began scribbling stories at a very early age, and in her teens she considered writing as a profession. But marriage and three daughters caused her to shelve that idea...for a while.

Then, rusty after so many years away from her writing, Yvonne enrolled in a fiction-writing course and set to work. She began with short stories and moved on to a novel, which took several months to complete. "Fortunately," she laughingly comments on her slow start, "I did not have to make a living out of my writing then. Otherwise, I would surely have starved!"

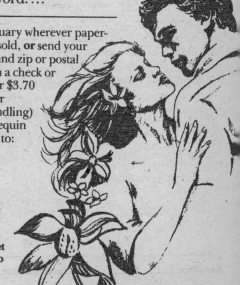

SUPERROMANCE

Longer, exciting, sensuous and dramatic!

Fascinating love stories that will hold
you in their magical spell till the last page
is turned!

Now's your chance to discover the earlier
books in this exciting series. Choose from
the great selection on the following page!

Choose from this list of great

SUPERROMANCES!

SUPERROMANCE

Complete and mail this coupon today!
